THE GUARDIAN SERIES
THE PURPLE DOOR
BOOK ONE

Janifer C. De Vos

Illustrations by
Gwendolyn Babbitt

Portland, Oregon

Edited by Deena Davis
Cover design by Bruce DeRoos

THE PURPLE DOOR

Published by Multnomah Press
Portland, Oregon 97266

Multnomah Press is a ministry of Multnomah School of the Bible, 8435 N.E. Glisan Street, Portland, Oregon 97220.

Printed in the United States of America

Library of Congress Cataloging-in-Publication Data

De Vos, Janifer C.
The purple door / Janifer C. De Vos : illustrations by Gwendolyn Babbitt.
p. cm.
Summary: When she accidentally falls through the purple door of an antiques shop. Erin embarks on an adventure which tests her commitment to God.
ISBN 0-88070-348-2
[1. Fantasy. 2. Christian life—Fiction.] I. Babbitt, Gwendolyn, ill. II. Title
PZ7.D4995 Pu 1990
[Fic]—dc20 90-32239
CIP
AC

90 91 92 93 94 95 - 6 5 4 3 2 1

Dedicated with love to my brother, Bruce,
who started this whole
story-telling
business!

Contents

Floorplans for
Antiques, Antiquities, Inc.

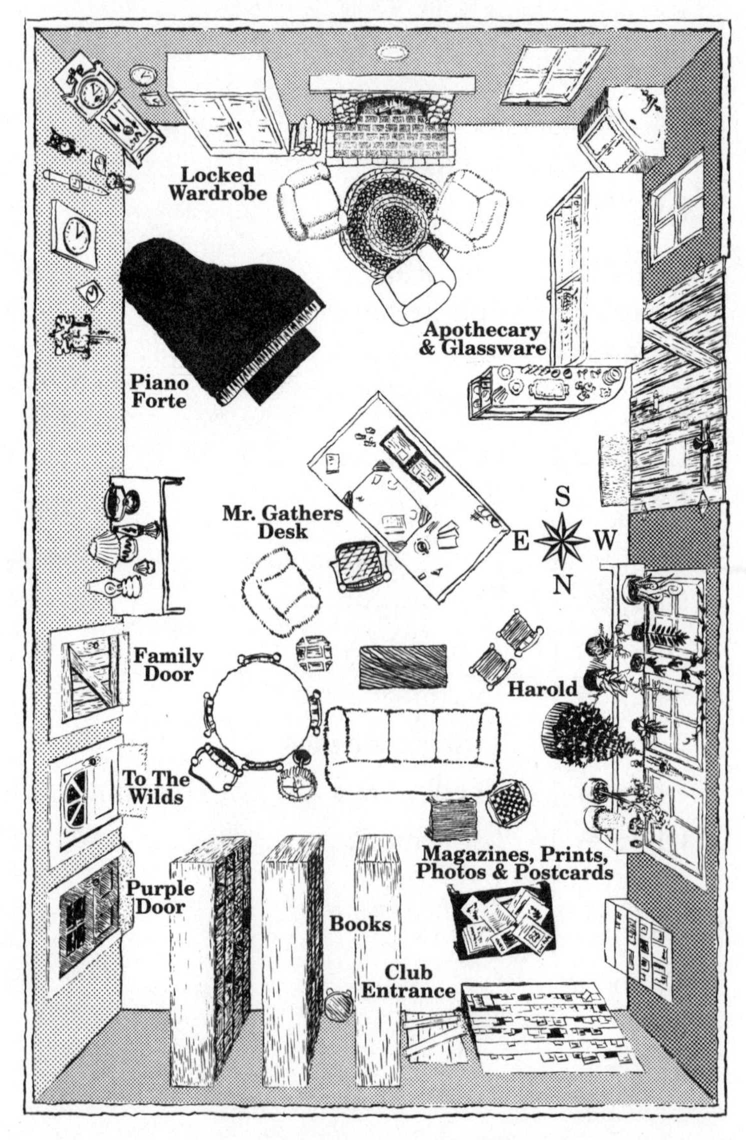

Map illustration by Brian Ray Davis

Prologue

The Council sat expectantly around the highly polished table. They all smiled encouragingly at the distinguished gentleman standing before them.

He cleared his throat and spoke:

"You have listened carefully to my recommendation that we wait no longer to fill the vacancy in our circle of active guardians. The Kingdom needs front-line replacements now. I propose we extend an invitation to my granddaughter to take the place I have vacated on earth." He looked from face to face with intensity. "I call the Council to a vote."

"I second the call," an angel to the gentleman's left responded.

"All in favor, say aye."

The room's domed ceiling echoed with the positive response.

"Any opposed?" asked the moderator.

There was silence.

The angel who had seconded the call to vote spoke again. "We will begin our preparations immediately."

The heavenly host rose together to adjourn, and the resounding "Amen" echoed to earth.

1
Prelude

ERIN GRIMLY RACED up the gravel driveway, her cheeks glowing red from the cold wind. She took two of the four back steps at a leap and came whirling in the door. "I'm home!"

"I'm in the dining room," a voice answered.

Erin put her stack of assorted books and notebooks on the drop-leaf kitchen table and pushed through the swinging door to the dining room. Her mother's latest writing project was spread out all over the table.

"So, how was school today?"

Erin pulled out one of the ladderback chairs and sat down next to her mother, who reached over to push a loose strand of brown hair out of Erin's eyes. Lately, Erin's hair had become a subject of heated discussion around the Grimly house. Long and straight, it looked lovely in a ponytail, and her bangs framed her oval face nicely, but Erin was rapidly growing to resent the pulled-back look and longed for curls. Unfortunately, set curls lasted all of ten minutes in her hair, and her father was still convinced that a perm was an unnecessary expense.

"School was okay. I had some homework in math, but Arnold helped me during study time. And I'm reading this great book for my next book report." Erin looked at the scattered manuscript on the table. "But it's probably not as good as yours." She pushed up the wire-rimmed glasses that had slid down her nose.

Mrs. Grimly laughed. "Such loyalty. Well, if you've done most of your homework, why not have a snack, get your practicing done, and go outside for a while? Just be sure you dress warmly enough." Mrs. Grimly gave her work an appraising glance. "I still have at least an hour's worth of writing to do here."

Erin headed for the kitchen, got out the peanut butter and matzos, and made a gooey cracker sandwich. Walking downstairs to her father's studio, she sat down at the upright piano to practice. Erin and the piano had a kind of love-hate relationship. Music held a special place in Erin's heart, and in Erin's family, too, for that matter. Her father was a music professor at the local community college, and she carried on the tradition of music in the form of piano lessons, talent present or not. It frustrated her to have heard wonderful music all her life, and to know what the music of Bach and Mozart was supposed to sound like, but not be able to play the pieces perfectly herself. Erin's Bach two-part inventions held inventions of her own that probably caused J. S. Bach to turn over in his grave.

Erin's long fingers rested comfortably on the white keys of the piano, and she quickly started the technique exercises she always used to warm up her fingers and her brain. Twice she stopped to impatiently tuck in stray wisps of hair from her long brown ponytail. Then came the pieces she was presently working on. She loved the effects she could create with the three brass foot pedals, but her teacher, Miss Rob, was forever telling her not to use too much of a good thing.

Practicing finally done, Erin ran back upstairs, changed into blue jeans and a warm sweatshirt, then headed out into the delicious freedom of idle time in the afternoon. She knew exactly how she planned to spend it, too. Walking up the hill through the grass of her backyard she came to a rockpile her dad had started several years ago during one of his many gardening projects. He had built a kind of wall along the short stretch of rusted barbed wire fence that separated that corner of the backyard from the field beyond, in an effort to at least partially hide the rusty fence from view. Erin teetered precariously but expertly on the rock wall, found a toehold, and swung her leg over carefully so as not to tear her jeans on the spiky barbed wire. Her destination was just ahead and to the right:

an abandoned barn, left over from another era when her neighborhood had been rural. She and two friends, Connie Smading and Arnold Lorenzo, used it as a kind of clubhouse, since it now stood abandoned. Mr. Lorenzo, an engineer, had inspected it and declared it safe for their occupancy.

Once over the fence, Erin looked up at the peculiar sloping roof. Erin's great-grandfather had designed just such a barn for his farm in the Netherlands. She walked past the large boarded-up double doors in front and came around the side to the little door that was their entrance. Mrs. Grimly said this entrance had probably been used when the farmer did his milking in the winter. That way most of the warm air stayed inside the barn.

When Erin stepped over the high threshold, it took several seconds for her eyes to adjust to the dim light that filtered through the cracks and the glass of the dirty windows on the northwest side of the barn. No one else had arrived yet, so Erin pulled up one of the three packing crates she and her friends used as chairs and sat down. As she looked around the barn's interior, she tried to imagine what must have gone on in that place a hundred years ago. The east wall was dark and solid with large nails hammered part way into the wall here and there to hold farm tools and harnesses. The north wall was divided by deep stalls built for cows and horses, Erin guessed; and even though she had attempted to sweep the dirt floor clean, there were still remnants of straw scattered at that end of the room. The west end of the barn was brightened somewhat by the light let in by three small windows. Years of dirt caked them—inside and out. They were too high for Erin to reach without a ladder, so they remained in this sad condition. Farther down the wall, someone had also cut a regular-sized door in one of the double door panels for more direct access.

The south wall interested Erin the most. Someone had tried to convert the barn into a studio apartment and had built a fireplace in the middle of the wall. The loft area had been torn out altogether. That was as far as the conversion idea had gone though.

"Hey, four-eyes!" a teasing voice called as the little side door opened. The voice was followed by a medium-height boy of about eleven. His brown hair and his clothing were of almost military regulation neatness.

"Arnold, I wish you would find another pet name for me. 'Four-eyes' is beginning to wear a bit thin." Erin's glasses were another sensitive subject with her these days. Her parents had agreed to contact lenses if she financed the greater part of the purchase. Unfortunately, babysitting money, plus her allowance, wasn't even enough to cover the cost of trips to the movies and the mall, let alone this contact lens dream of hers. She felt very discouraged.

"Arnold Lorenzo, put your wisecracking in neutral," a new voice commanded. Connie Smading came through the side door just a few seconds behind Arnold. Pulling the door shut behind her, she slid the crosspiece through the wooden runners to keep the door closed and their meeting place private. Connie was a little taller than Erin. She too wore her long blond hair in a ponytail and dreamed of curls. She came over and stood next to Erin, squinting slightly to see better in the dimness. "This place seems different today. Do you guys notice anything?" She looked quizzically at her friends.

Arnold sauntered around the room and came over to join Erin on the packing crates. "I see today what I have seen every day for the last four or five years we've played in here: dirt floor, gray walls, dirty windows, and a crazy ceiling." He leaned back with both hands holding firmly to the front of his crate, the balls of his feet pressed hard against the ground. Slowly he tipped the crate back until he was precariously balanced, barely touching the wall. Suddenly he flung both hands out and remained suspended in mid-air with the crate tilting crazily.

"Ta-dah!"

"Better be careful, Arn. You're in the perfect position for a push." Erin reached teasingly in his direction. Arnold hastily brought the crate down.

"Come on, Connie. What could be different?" Erin turned to her friend. "We're the only ones who care anything about this place. We're the only people who ever even come in here. Come to think of it, I bet no adult has been in here since Arnold's dad inspected this place when we first discovered it." Erin stopped talking and looked around thoughtfully. In spite of what she'd just said there was something different . . . but what was it?

"Arnold, are you humming?" Erin asked with suspicious annoyance. "I hear music."

For once, the usually mischievous Arnold looked genuinely surprised. "No, I'm not."

"Oh, come on, you two," said Connie. "Don't play games about this."

"Sh!" Erin held up a warning hand. She got up from her crate to locate the source of the music. As it grew louder, she recognized a Bach two-part invention—*the one she had been practicing earlier that afternoon.*

"This is spooky. Let's get out of here." Connie made for the door. Arnold was right behind her and reached out to help her unbolt it. Erin remained in the center of the room, turning in a slow circle to hear where the sound was coming from. The clear notes of a piano grew louder as she circled toward the fireplace.

"Come on, Erin. Let's go." Arnold called from outside.

The music suddenly stopped as mysteriously as it had started.

"Erin!" Connie shouted.

Erin reluctantly followed her friends and stepped across the threshold, shading her eyes from the sunlight.

"Do you hear anything out here?" Erin asked the two. They shook their heads. "It could have been someone's stereo system or a radio." But she felt her own sense of doubt in that explanation. The music had definitely come from inside the barn.

"Well, I'm going home." Arnold started walking through the field in the direction of his house. "Don't expect to see too much of me around here any more, girls. I've decided that I've outgrown this clubhouse stuff." Turning to face them, now walking backwards, he shouted, "See you at school tomorrow. The boys are going to win the kickball game, Erin. Better wash your glasses tonight so you'll have all four eyes to see the ball." Laughing at his own joke, he almost fell when he came unexpectedly to the sidewalk.

Erin glared after him as he turned and sauntered down the next street.

"Ignore him, Erin." Connie spoke kindly to her friend. "You know," she continued thoughtfully, "Arnold is getting more obnoxious by the minute. He never used to be like that. I could use a little vacation from his big mouth. I'm glad he wants out of the club."

Erin stood in the tall grass next to the rockpile and felt the prickles of anger and embarrassment subside. "What's bad, Connie, is that his teasing is starting to get to me. I used to be able to ignore him. But now some of the other kids are following his lead. Oh, contact lenses, here I come!"

"I've got to get going, kid. I hear my long division homework calling me." The two girls climbed back over the fence and the rocks, walked down the sloping hill to Erin's back door, and parted company at the driveway.

Later that night, Erin had difficulty falling asleep even after reading a chapter in her latest mystery, her mind filled with fantasies of defeating the boys in the next day's kickball game and a lingering curiosity about Bach in the barn. Finally she turned over one last time and fell asleep.

2
When It Began

THE HIGH POINT of the next school day was the kickball game at ten o'clock recess. The girls took the boys' team totally by surprise and got the only two runs before the bell rang. Shouting, "We're number one!" the girls happily trotted off the field while the boys departed in stunned silence, dragging their feet. They hadn't even made it infield. Connie and Erin waited just long enough to get Arnold's attention, then flashed him a triumphant smile.

The rest of the school day was covered with the rosy glow of success for the girls. Erin walked home from school smiling all the way. After telling her mother about the kickball victory and fortifying herself with a sandwich, she practiced for thirty minutes, and then decided to go sit in the barn for awhile. She was hoping she would hear the mysterious music again.

Once outside, Erin looked up at the sky. The wintry afternoon hung grey and dripping on the clothesline of January. She stepped carefully on the large cement stepping stones that went up the hill of her backyard. They didn't lead anywhere in particular. . . . As a matter of fact, if you walked up them with your eyes closed, you'd run smack into the horse apple tree.

There was a strange smell in the air. Erin sniffed again. Smoke? Now where would smoke be coming from? Nobody had leaves to burn this time of year. Then she spotted it. A thin wisp of smoke curled from the chimney of the barn.

Erin raced to the back fence. She expected to see what she always saw: one very old barn. But this time that's not what she saw at all.

"Come on, Erin," she said to herself. "Must have been that cucumber and cream cheese sandwich you had." She looked again, peering tensely through the thick lenses of her glasses.

It was still there. Someone had done some major repair work on the barn. The double doors were no longer boarded up, and they had been painted white. A lovely coat of red paint covered the barn's exterior, and the windowpanes glimmered clean in the grey day.

"Now, Erin, my dear," she said to herself. "Look carefully . . ." She closed her eyes and then opened them. "Still there? Hmmmmmm . . ."

There was a small, old-fashioned sign hanging from a black wrought-iron arm above the double doors:

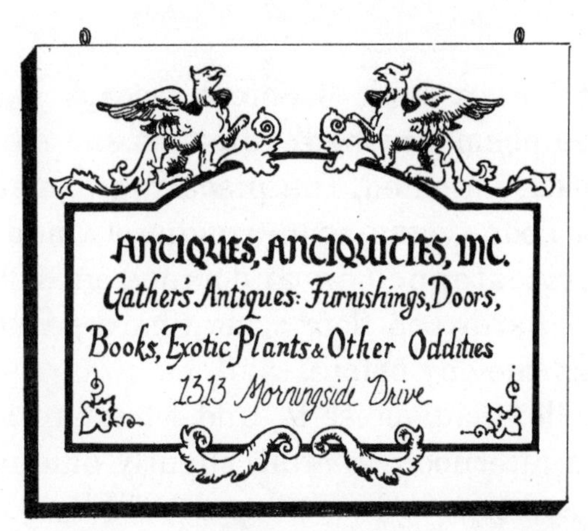

"Doors? Exotic plants?" Erin wondered. "I've been antique shopping with Mom before but never to a place with antique doors or exotic plants!"

And in one window a sign read:

Shop Help Wanted
Curious Apply Within

Help wanted! Erin's thoughts whirled. She could really use some extra cash to supplement her babysitting funds. Maybe contact lenses weren't so far out of reach after all.

Erin walked to the newly painted white doors. There was a small placard nailed to the center of the regular-sized door built into the left double panel. She read:

'Tis the afternoon to begin,
A new job is waiting
So come right______.

"In," Erin said, "Come right IN. But why isn't the poem finished?" Just as she said "in," the words vanished, the placard gleamed gold, and the door swung open, ringing a small tinkly bell. Erin stepped in and stood on a highly polished hardwood floor where hard-packed dirt had been the day before.

"Hello, mademoiselle, and what can I do for you this afternoon?" A tall, slightly balding man peered at her over his spectacles. "Why have you come?" He asked the question with a slight smile that seemed to add a warm glow to his countenance.

Erin was so overwhelmed by the barn's transformation that she couldn't answer for a moment. Then, realizing the old gentleman was waiting for a reply, she said the first thing that came to mind.

"I'm here because I was curious," Erin answered, her mind flashing back to the sign in the window.

"Very good. I am Mr. Gather, a modest keeper of things old, older, and oldest. And this," he gestured in one sweeping motion with his pencil, "is my shop."

Erin saw neatly arranged collections of bottles and dishes directly to her right; shelves and shelves of books now lined the stalls on the north wall; potted plants were growing under the

high windows. Firewood was stacked neatly next to the fireplace. A row of closed wooden doors ran along the east wall. There was a beautiful pianoforte in the southeast corner of the spacious room.

"To work here, Miss . . . Miss . . . what is your name?"

"Erin," she said. "Erin Grimly."

"To work here, Miss Grimly, you must know your alphabet—the Roman one, of course. The Chinese one is much more descriptive but entirely too complicated. Each individual collection is organized alphabetically. Without that we would have chaos. Have you ever tried to find, say, pickled phantom fangs among one thousand other items without a system?"

Mr. Gather stopped speaking for a moment. He walked over to a large book hanging from a nail next to the front door.

"This," he said, "is GATHER'S GUIDE FOR SHOPPERS. All the contents of my store, plus items to order, are here. I'll give you until Saturday to learn the shop and a little bit about the GUIDE'S contents. You strike me as a promising apprentice."

3
First Day

ERIN HAD GONE home that night with her thoughts in a mad whirl. During school the next day, she could hardly concentrate on the work in front of her. When she finally returned to Antiques, Antiquities, Inc. the next afternoon, she looked around eagerly. The shop made her very fingertips tingle with curiosity, her mind filled with questions of the "how," "when," and "where" variety. Mr. Gather was about to greet Erin when the front door opened, ringing the bell once again.

"Bonjour, Monsieur Gather! Comment allez-vous?"

"Ah, Madame Mer, très bien, merci."

Mr. Gather left Erin and waited on his latest customer, a tall, attractive Frenchwoman. This gave Erin a chance to wander around unsupervised.

Her eye was caught again by the row of brightly painted doors on the back wall, so she quickly appraised the variety of apothecary jars containing liquids and powders, the lush green of the botanical section, the packed book stalls (she'd come back here later), and stopped in front of the doors. Each door had a booklet hanging from its brass knob. The orange door attracted her attention first, and she reached for its accompanying slender booklet hanging from a matching orange ribbon. "The Family Door as Explored by Zacharias Gather," was neatly penned on the cover. Inside it read:

> *Friends, do you need a break from your everyday responsibilities? Do you just need a good laugh? Then come through the Family Door. See the human equation at its best and funniest. For one hour each trip, family entertainment can be yours. Entrance every sixty minutes, earth time.*

"Crazy!" thought Erin. "I wonder how these things work?"

The door to the left of the Family Door was deep green, and the accompanying booklet was large. "Door to the the Wilds: A Jungle Experience as Explored by Zacharias Gather." The advertisement inside went like this:

> *Friends, do you long for the beautiful music of the night-howling hyenas? Do your nightmares lack that touch of nature found only in a good jungle? Are you ready to leave the rat race for a simpler way of life? If you answered yes to any of the above*

questions, take the twenty-four-hour trip through the Door to the Wilds. (This door is not recommended for children under twelve due to mature subject matter in some tribal customs, such as head shrinking.) Entrance every thirty minutes, earth time.

Erin eagerly continued on to a small purple door at the end of the row. The window glass was smokey, the knob unpolished, and it had no key. Its booklet had only one page, written in beautiful longhand. She read:

This door has not been sufficiently explored to make it available on the market as yet. Exploration by Mr. Gather will be forthcoming as time and the door permit.

Erin held the booklet thoughtfully in her fingers.

"So, Miss Grimly, you've progressed to the Doors," Mr. Gather's voice broke into her thoughts. "Each is for rent." Mr. Gather stopped speaking long enough to smile and wave good-bye to Madame Mer and then turned to Erin and continued. "Most of my customers you will find delightful. There is one customer, however, you must be a bit cautious around, my dear. Her name is Miranda Banushta. She is what she appears to be . . . and more." Mr. Gather was silent for a moment, gently stroking his pencil while he stared thoughtfully into space.

"Mr. Gather, where did . . . how did you . . . I was here the day before yesterday, and this place—-" Erin was momentarily distracted by a thick length of twine on the floor in front of her, and she bent down to pick it up. In mid-reach she drew her hand back in surprise. The rope moved! Back and forth, back and forth it went. It reminded Erin of a cat's tail twitching angrily.

"Parenthesis, how nice of you to come early today." Mr. Gather was talking to someone, but Erin couldn't see anyone else in the shop. He looked briefly in her direction. "This is Miss Grimly. She may fill the clerk's position. Miss Grimly, may I present the distinguished feline extraordinaire, Parenthesis."

Erin followed Mr. Gather's gaze and still saw nothing. Nothing except the twitching rope which now hung in a curve in the air. It was coming toward her. Suddenly Erin saw more than rope. About two feet away, a head with little ears and long whiskers appeared. Finally, four paws and a body filled the space between head and tail. A cat! Parenthesis was a cat!

Mr. Gather reached down, picked Parenthesis up, and walked purposefully to a small saucer in the corner by the front door. Placing

the white cat in front of it, he stood up, smiling ever so slightly.

"She dearly loves her little afternoon snack of sautéed bat brains. We import them from Australia."

"Parenthesis. That's an interesting name for a cat," said Erin. She wanted to say something about the cat's unusual appearance but wasn't sure she'd actually seen what she thought she had seen.

"You will find, my dear Miss Grimly, that names of things often explain a great deal about them. In this cat's case, her name explains one of her many talents: materializing and de-materializing, one section of herself at a time. She always starts with the two ends and leaves the middle for last, reminiscent of English parentheses. Hence . . . her name. She is an orphan from behind the purple door about which you were reading a moment ago."

Erin looked at the beautiful white cat with new interest. Parenthesis had finished her snack and was busily cleaning her silky ears. Erin longed to pick the cat up, but something held her back. Parenthesis didn't seem the kind of cat one spoke to or petted without permission from the cat first!

The bell over the front door rang out again. Erin turned swiftly with Mr. Gather to answer its ring. There in the doorway stood a large, colorfully dressed woman with long brown naturally curly hair.

"Oh, Mr. Gather, I'm soooo glad I dropped in and found you here. I'd be soooo disappointed if I had missed you. You doooo have that new door ready for me—-YOU PROMISED, you know. I simply must have the purple one. I've rented all the others you have in stock." She stopped talking, her gaze falling on Erin. "And what's this?" she asked sarcastically.

"Madam Banushta, this is Miss Erin Grimly. She is here learning more about the clerk's position." Mr. Gather continued in a resigned voice, "Miss Grimly, may I present Madam Miranda Banushta, scientist cum laude."

GUIDE FOR
SHOPPERS

"That's summa cum laude, Gather darling. Now about that door. Do I get it? You know payment is no object. And tell me, is this Grimly-thing for sale? I've never had one, and it might prove to be interesting."

"Madam Banushta, neither the door, nor the 'Grimly-thing' as you so rudely put it, is for sale. As Guardian of the Doors, I am not allowed to rent one I have not thoroughly explored myself. The purple door has behind it a mystery not to be taken lightly. It is my first door out of this world, and it must be handled with utmost care. I will be most happy to show you something else."

Madam Banushta turned away from them and strolled haughtily through the shop, her nose at a snooty angle. She gave a huge sigh of boredom as she stopped to leaf through GATHER'S GUIDE FOR SHOPPERS. Then she saw Parenthesis sitting on the sill of one of the high shop windows, busily cleaning her whiskers.

"Heeeerrrrrreeeeee, kitty, kitty! Coommee, pussy!"

Madam Banushta walked over to the window sill and looked up only to find it empty. "Wh-what?" She spun around, glared at Erin and looked at her feet. "How dare you play tricks with me, Grimly-thing!" she spat accusingly.

Confused, Erin looked down and jumped because there was a head, tail, and four paws next to her feet!

"Mister Gather! Be assured such impudence will have consequences!" Miranda pulled a flat, black rectangular panel out of her pocket and pushed two buttons on the left corner. A soft humming sound filled the room, and quite suddenly Miranda Banushta was gone. Erin stared in amazement at the empty air where Madam had stood seconds before.

"Where did she go—how did she go? Oh, Mr. Gather, I'm sorry if I've caused a problem."

"Miranda has constructed a device that enables her to enjoy limited interdimensional earth travel. She seems to think she can go wherever she wishes, whenever she wishes. Do not be concerned. Her threats are usually without teeth." He bent down, picked up Parenthesis, and tickled her under the chin. The cat lay contentedly, purring loudly. "Since you are an earth child, when, may I ask, will you be coming again?"

Erin was momentarily distracted by being called "an earth child." "I could come for sure tomorrow from 3:30 to 5:00," she said. "I'll have to discuss this with my mom and dad before I commit to a schedule."

"Very good. We shall expect you tomorrow at 3:30. And Miss Grimly, be prompt. We have a lot to do. Since this is a trial period, we will give you something from the shop as payment for your services rather than give you cash." He smiled at her, eyes twinkling. "Saturday morning we shall decide formally if you are suited to us and we to you. Good day, Miss Grimly. God go with you."

All the way home, Erin thought about everything she'd seen. After hanging up her jacket, she flopped down on her bed and closed her eyes, trying to visualize the shop again. Suddenly, she sat up. Had she just heard the sound of the little bell that hung above the shop door? Impossible. But then she saw a neat little package on her dresser that hadn't been there a minute before. There was a card attached.

To: Miss E. Grimly
From: Antiques, Antiquities, Inc.
For: One Afternoon's Work

Erin took the box to her bed and opened it carefully. Inside was a small pot with a tiny plant in it. Instructions accompanied it.

Water me once a day,
Talk to me before you play.
Then I will surely grow for you,
And I will certainly glow for you
The whole night through.
—The Nightus Lightus plant.

Erin felt a little dazed . . .

"Exotic plants . . . doors leading to other places . . . a cat who can disappear and reappear in sections . . . people who disappear and reappear . . . Wow, this is some antique shop, that's for sure. Now, I've got to think out a really good way to break all this to Mom and Dad. Some of it they won't believe," thought Erin as she stroked the leaves of her new plant. "Some of it even I don't believe! I want them to say," she imitated her father's baritone, "'Why of course you may have this little job, Erin. It sounds fascinating.'"

Fortunately for Erin, her parents went to the opera early that evening and slept in the following morning so she had more time to plan out and rehearse her convincing speech.

4
Jungle Excursion

WHEN ERIN ARRIVED at school the next day, she was all set to tell Connie about the barn's amazing transformation, but as it turned out Connie was at home, for the second day in a row, with a terrible cold. Arnold was still bent out of shape over the kickball game and avoided Erin all day.

When the dismissal bell rang, Erin quickly gathered her belongings and scurried out the classroom door. She wanted to get home in plenty of time to do her piano practicing and arrive on schedule at Antiques, Antiquities, Inc. She made it to the rockpile wall at precisely 3:28 and scrambled over, catching her skirt on the wire fence. At 3:29, she was standing at the front door of the shop. Today the placard read:

Winter-humdrum-humbug.
Grey sky, wind, and thundrug.
Ugh. Winter. Humdrum. Hum____.

"Bug!" said Erin loudly to be sure she was heard. Much to her relief, the placard gleamed gold, the door swung open, and the bell announced her entrance.

"Precisely 3:30 P.M., Miss Grimly. Excellent. I

trust your day has thus far been pleasant?"

"Very pleasant, Mr. Gather," said Erin, "and thank you for my Nightus Lightus plant."

"I'm glad you found it amusing. Now, I want you to handle at least two customers today on your own. So I suggest you browse through the shop so you will be familiar with our inventory. After all, you cannot suggest items to customers if you don't know what we have, now can you?"

"No, sir." Erin walked slowly around the display cabinets and shelves near the front door. At one point she seemed to be in a kind of apothecary section of ancient medicines. There was a row of herbal teas and tonics on one shelf along with small containers labelled "Crow's Beaks for stronger fingernails," and several jars labelled "Balm of Gilead" on another. The apothecary was located next to a deep porcelain sink with copper faucets. "Maybe all this comes under the heading of 'oddities,'" she thought.

Next, the plants. It was almost like walking into a greenhouse. Potted plants of varying sizes were neatly arranged in rows under the high windows set in the west wall. Erin was surprised and pleased to discover that the three crates the children had used for chairs had been set in strategic sitting spots. Near her crate a tall evergreen tree was growing. The top brushed the shop's ceiling. She was reaching out to touch the

Christmas tree-like needles when she heard Parenthesis growl nearby. Erin turned to see what was upsetting the cat as Mr. Gather hurried over, frowning. Parenthesis peered down from one of the window sills, giving her low warning growl again.

"Miss Grimly, I neglected to warn you about Harold, the omnivorous conifer. He looks innocent, but his needles hold a great deal of pain for humans."

Erin decided she'd had enough of the plants for a while. She walked on to the over-stacked cow stall shelves holding hundreds of volumes—some thin, some thick, in assorted colors, all very dusty. The gilt letters on a brown leather spine caught her eye, and she pulled it carefully off the shelf.

"Missstttterrr Gather." The words hung haughtily in the air. Erin recognized the voice. She sighed, put down the book she held, and started searching for some sign of Miranda. The atmosphere by the wall of ticking clocks began to blur. Madam Banushta soon stood before them.

"Well, Madam, is there something you need?" Mister Gather asked shortly.

"You really don't carry anything I *need*. However, my nerves could use a bit of soothing after all the experimenting I've been doing lately. I enjoyed the Jungle Door tremendously earlier."

She took several steps in the door's direction. "When will it be available?"

"It's quite free for use now, if you like." Mr. Gather went to the green door, took the oversized key and inserted it in the lock. There was a click and a creak as the wood frame door swung inward.

"You see, Miss Grimly, the world beyond this door is constantly turning. Therefore, since earth rotates on its axis every twenty-four hours, our shop entrance is turning at that speed, too. Only when the door's entrance lines up with our entrance are we able to go through. Sometimes the doors' entrances meet, but do not meet exactly, and earth feels it in the form of sudden winds, dark clouds, or turbulent weather." Mr. Gather reached out and opened the door's travel folder to show Erin the door entrance diagram.

Miranda turned to Erin in surprise. "Why, Grimly-thing! You mean you've not gone door-hopping?" Miranda was incredulous. "You mmmussst go! You simply must accompany me. Gather! How can your little clerk effectively explain the doors to your patrons if she hasn't been through one? IMMMMpossible!"

Mr. Gather gazed suspiciously over Erin's head at Miranda. Erin wanted very much to go. She just wished someone besides Miranda had invited her. Looking past Mr. Gather into the

Jungle doorway, she saw nothing but blackness.

"Well, Mr. Gather, are you going to allow your clerk-to-be to accompany me or not?"

The opening was turning from black to deep purple, like a new day dawning. Erin looked at Mr. Gather anxiously.

"You have approximately two minutes and ten seconds remaining before departure," said a feminine mechanical voice from inside the door.

"Miss Grimly, you may accompany Madam Banushta if you wish. And Madam, Miss Grimly is to be back at 5:00 P.M. today. Precisely 5:00 P.M."

"The entrance interlock is now forty-five seconds away," the computer voice said.

"What do I do?" asked Erin excitedly.

"Just walk through," replied Miranda impatiently.

The colors of the door's entrance were as

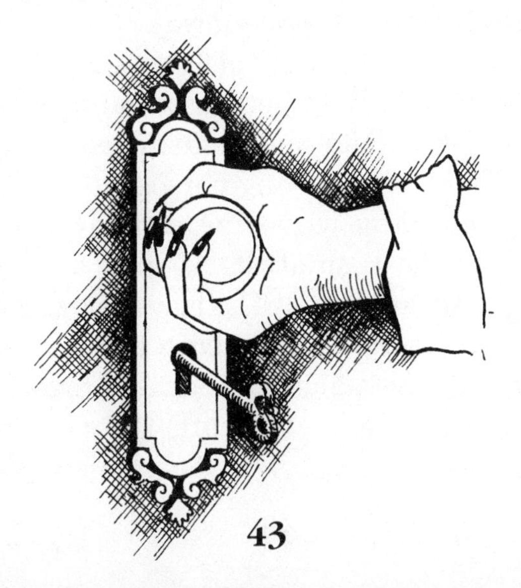

bright as day now. Erin saw another world stretching out before her on the other side of the green door frame.

"Now!" commanded Mr. Gather. "Have a good trip!"

Erin stepped through the door right behind Madam Banushta. She took another step forward and was horrified to find nothing underneath her feet to support her weight. She began falling quite rapidly through a dense growth of trees when a large palm frond slid under her and began propelling her forward about ten feet above ground.

"A palm buggy," Erin thought to herself. "How ingenious!"

The trees gradually thinned out, and Erin found herself hovering over the banks of a large, swiftly moving river. Another figure fluttered at the same altitude a few feet away.

"Grimly-thing! I say, isn't this absolutely the most primitive way of getting around? Can you believe it?" Miranda shouted sarcastically. But she did seem to be enjoying herself.

The two palm leaves zipped toward what appeared to be a small dock with a river rig resting quietly at its end. The leaves slowed down, lowered, and at three feet above the boat's deck, tilted sideways, sending Miranda and Erin flying.

Brushing themselves off, the two jungle

explorers surveyed their surroundings. Erin heard sounds all around her— multitudes of bird voices, winds whispering through many treetops; was that a lion's roar? She looked around quickly to be sure Madam Banushta was close at hand. Even Miranda's company was welcome here.

"Oh, yes. Oh, yes. Welcome aboard Victoria II, Victoria II. Some explorers! Lovely! Where to, ladies? Where to?" A lanky, well-tanned, somewhat elderly gentleman came from behind a deck chair.

"Where's the man in charge?" demanded Madam Banushta.

"I am, I am indeed the man in charge. My name is Captain Captain."

"We're here for an abbreviated jungle cruise. This child has to be back to Gather's Antiques at 5:00 P.M., earth time. That means we have less than two hours to enjoy this, so get moving," she snapped rudely.

The captain started the motor, and the craft chugged slowly into the main current of the dark green waters. The surroundings reminded Erin of an old Tarzan movie. An occasional mosquito buzzed in her ear. The motor purred rhythmically, relaxingly, and she felt herself sliding into a comfortable twilight doze.

Suddenly Miranda let out such a screech that Erin jumped right out of her chair. "I want one! Grimly-thing, come look! Captain! Stop the boat. Stop, I say. Oh, I must have one. I simply must have one of those little creatures."

Erin came around the side of the deck to see what all the excitement was about. Madam Banushta was scrambling down the boat's ladder, and the captain was hurrying to stop her, yelling, "No one leaves the vessel! No one leaves! You know the rules, the rules!"

Captain Captain grabbed one of Madam's chubby arms and pulled with all his feeble strength. Madam Banushta was hovering over the murky water, beating the old man with her purse.

"I want one! I want one!"

"No one leaves the vessel. No one! No one!"

As the comical struggle continued, none of the boaters noticed that the now-pilotless craft had completely turned around and was heading straight for the pier from which they had started.

Erin was pulling the captain who was pulling Miranda. After several heaves, the two succeeded in getting the hefty scientist back up the top rungs of the ladder and on deck.

"Madam! The rules! The rules!" Captain Captain scolded. He stopped short, turned pale, and began a new shriek, "My boat! My boat!"

The vessel was relentlessly chugging straight toward shore. Captain Captain flew to the ship's wheel, spun it hard to one side and frantically blew the boat's whistle even though there appeared to be no one on shore to heed the warning. The Victoria jerked a hard left, but it was too late.

Erin wasn't sure which sensation she perceived first: the sound of splintering wood when the boat plowed through the pier, the crash of ship against shore that caused her to hit the deck and skin her knee, or the wetness of the river spray as it splashed over the Victoria II's sides.

"Grimly-thing! This is all your fault! I never should have taken an inept juvenile door-hopping. It must be 5:00 by now. Let's go."

The somewhat confused Erin watched as Madam Banushta purposefully picked her way through the wrecked pier's broken boards which were now piled haphazardly on the deck of the boat. Captain Captain sobbed softly at the bow. She reached over his bent head and pressed a red button marked EARLY DEPARTURES. EMERGENCIES ONLY.

In one big "swoosh" Erin found herself dumped like a heap of rags on Mr. Gather's floor. Madam Banushta was nowhere to be seen. The adventure had apparently been cut short. Mr. Gather came from the bookstalls with a feather duster in his hand.

"Why, Miss Grimly! It's hardly 4:30! What happened?"

Before Erin could answer, she heard a shrill whistle and a rusty creak, like a mailbox opening and then closing.

"Excuse me. Special Delivery letter." Mr. Gather walked to the green Jungle Door. A white envelope lay on the floor underneath the mail slot. Erin noticed it looked a little wet. Mr. Gather opened it and read silently.

"Oh, my." He took a deep breath, exhaled and scratched his nose thoughtfully. "Second time for this door. One of these days she will go too far."

Erin had a good idea who "she" was. Mr. Gather hung a sign on the Jungle Door: "Closed for repairs."

Erin collected her thoughts. "This happened before, Mr. Gather?" She recalled the ship's name, Victoria II. "Was there a Victoria I?"

Mr. Gather sat down on one of the clubhouse crates near a banana tree and dusted the large leaves. "Miss Grimly, last month there was a Victoria I and a very capable captain. After Madam Banushta rented the door, there was no Victoria I, the captain quit, and my insurance for all the doors doubled."

"Mr. Gather, if Miranda can travel around with this gadget she's invented, why does she even want to use your doors?"

"Good question, Miss Grimly. Whatever her

reasons, I think her ultimate goal is to gain access to the purple door, and that I cannot allow. She must never be allowed behind that door." He looked the sternest Erin had ever seen him look. "She is one customer I will always wait on."

"No problem there!"

Erin sat thoughtfully on the floor. A tail and some whiskers floated through the air toward her. The white cat materialized next to her fingers, demanding to be petted.

"Good afternoon, Parenthesis. Mr. Gather, have you given Parenthesis her snack today?"

Mr. Gather shook his head, put down the feather duster, and walked over behind the glassware displays and apothecary section. Parenthesis followed him, meowing all the way. He rinsed her dish in the sink and opened an ancient icebox Erin had not noticed before. Mr. Gather spooned the sautéed mixture into Parenthesis' dish and handed it to Erin over the cat's head. "You may do the honors." With great care, Erin put the dish in front of the cat, who began swallowing chunks hungrily.

"Parenthesis," Erin laughed, "you'll have to go on a diet soon. You're getting fat!"

"Miss Grimly, the Jungle Door catastrophe has caused me to almost forget to tell you the good tidings! I do believe Parenthesis is going to have kittens quite soon!"

Mr. Gather and Erin sat down among the plants. "You know, Mr. Gather, this is like sitting in the Garden of Eden. Everything is so lush and green." Erin breathed in the smells of rich earth and growing things.

Mr. Gather appraised the greenery around him. "These are lovely selected specimens of what was growing there, but hardly completely representative."

Erin looked at him in amazement. "You mean you got these plants from the Garden of Eden?"

Mr. Gather answered her question with one of his own: "When do you plan to tell your parents about the shop and your clerking?" He spoke softly, with kind but firm inflection.

Erin was silent. She looked down at her hands. "I really haven't had the right moment in the last twenty-four hours," she answered honestly.

"It is written, 'Honor your father and mother.'" Mr. Gather looked at her. "A secret of this kind would not be honoring."

"I know, I know. But Mr. Gather, what happens if they say I can't come here and work?"

"Be obedient." Mr. Gather said the words slowly, softly, looking Erin straight in the eye.

"Yes, sir," she said and was surprised by the hope rising in her heart.

5
A Disquieting Appearance

IN ERIN'S THREE afternoons of visiting Antiques, Antiquities, Inc., she had gained an adequate working knowledge of the store's stock. Her room at home now contained two intriguing items from the antique shop, which continued sending the nightly special delivery packages. The delivery system was still a mystery.

Saturday afternoon, as she walked to her piano lesson, she slowly reviewed the inventory list. Today she'd either keep her job or lose it. She was, to be sure, very nervous.

"Alphabetically, alphabetically. Now let's see . . . hmmm. Arms and armor, autograph letters and documents, automatons." She jumped a crack in the sidewalk and continued her mental review. "B . . . Baroque music listings with over fifteen hundred entries for Bach . . . books . . . boxes . . ., C . . . C . . . Oh, nuts! I'm already here. C . . . crummy piano lessons."

Erin walked up the three steps, through the open french doors and sat down in the dusty parlor that served as a waiting room for Miss Rob's students. One of Miss Rob's redeeming features was a passionate love for animals, and one of her precious pets came to greet Erin.

The studio door opened, and as Erin bent to pat the fluffy kitten, she saw a handsome, dark haired young man walk past, listening intently to Miss Rob.

"Noah, you are sacrificing much in your neglect of technique. You must work harder on your minor scales."

"The minor scales, my Beethoven, and a little more Brahms for next time, I promise, my dear lady." The young man's voice was respectful, yet Erin could hear the smile in his words.

Miss Rob softened at the young man's response, gave him a little pat on the shoulder and a smile.

Young Noah was out the door and down the cement steps when Miss Rob turned to the reluctant Erin, took her by the shoulders, and steered her into the large, airy studio.

A little jewel-faced clock set on the music stand ticked away the forty-five minutes of her lesson. The mistakes grew more and more numerous as time went by. Finally the piano could rest. Erin fairly ran out the french doors, jumped the porch steps and got her thoughts back on the track of the alphabetical review of antiquities.

"Erin! Erin!" a voice called urgently behind her. She turned and saw Miss Rob coming rapidly toward her.

"Oh, no!" Erin thought. "She must have forgotten to tell me something. More practicing, I bet."

Miss Rob had a thick music book in her arms. Erin looked at it and felt a little sick.

"Erin, dear, this belongs to Mr. Sebastian, the young man who has his lesson right before you. He left this today. Could you take it to him? His address is one street over from yours. Here, I have his card." The little card was stuck like a bookmark in the well-worn music.

Erin was so relieved to find the music wasn't for her that she immediately took the card and book without even looking at either one. It wasn't until she reached her own street that she checked the address and gasped. In very ornate lettering and faded ink the little blue card read:

Mr. Noah Sebastian
1313 Morningside Drive

That was the address for Antiques, Antiquities, Inc. But she'd never seen him there. Well, she had to admit she hardly knew all there was to know about the shop. Still, who was he?

"How was your lesson, dear?" Her mother's voice called to her from the kitchen. Erin had been so filled with her own thoughts she hadn't even noticed she was standing on her own back porch. She came into the warm kitchen.

"Oh, okay. Mom, what time is dinner?"

"Early, why? Are you planning to be gone again this afternoon?" Erin's mother turned to her with a dishtowel in hand. "Erin, where have you been going the last couple afternoons? You and Arnold aren't spying on poor Mrs. Chloetilde again, are you? I know she does strange things, but I've told you children to stay away from there."

"No, ma'am. I haven't been spying." Erin was inwardly startled and momentarily distracted to hear the words "honor" and "obedient" echoing in her mind. She squared her shoulders resolutely and blurted out, "Mom, could we please have a family meeting tonight? There's something I'd like to talk over with you and Dad."

"Sure, honey. Is anything wrong?" Her mother's face showed her concern.

"No, don't worry. It's something good."

Her mother smiled and turning back to the towel rack, said over her shoulder, "By the way, cat lover, have you seen that gorgeous white cat that's been around here the last few days? This morning I was watching the cardinals out our back windows, and I saw this bushy white tail out of the corner of my eye. When I turned to look, a beautiful cat was sitting on our back fence." Her voice took on a more serious tone. "Erin, when did I get my glasses?"

"I think just a while ago. October?"

"That's what I thought. Hmmmm. I could have sworn there was only a white tail on that fence . . . and then . . . there was a cat. Strange, don't you think?" Her mother turned away and went back to cleaning up the kitchen.

Erin went to her room and collapsed on her bed in a fit of giggles. She rolled over and hugged her pajama-bag-cat-pillow and began thinking seriously about what she would say to her parents tonight.

The music book belonging to Mr. Sebastian was laying at the foot of Erin's bed and served as a reminder of where she had to be at 3:30. Her nervousness returned. Hopping off the quilted spread onto the hardwood floor, she reached for her jacket and the music book.

"Bye, Mom! See you later!" Erin swooshed past her mother, slammed the screen door, and felt the cold shivers of a winter afternoon creep swiftly inside the warmth of her clothes. She didn't mind though, knowing in a minute she'd be warm again.

The familiar barn door was tightly closed. Erin eagerly walked forward to read today's message:

Without me there are no ins or outs.
Would you climb in a window
to enter your house?

Of course not!
But do you know I can be more,
Much more, than wood and paint
though you see just a ____?

"Door," spoke Erin firmly. The plaque gleamed gold, and Erin walked through the open door.

Mr. Gather came from the back of the shop. "Precisely 3:30, as usual. Miss Grimly, I must tell you that your promptness is definitely a plus in favor of my hiring you."

He had been working by the doors, and had the large master key in his hand.

Erin had put down the music book and was hanging up her jacket.

"Mr. Gather," she said over her shoulder, "does a Mr. Noah Sebastian work here? My music teacher asked me to return this music book to him. His address is the same as the shop's."

Mr. Gather turned to answer her question just as a young man's cheerful baritone called out into the shop.

"Mr. G! Mr. G! Sorry I'm late, but I started on my new Beethoven and lost track of the time. You've got to hear what I can do so far."

A young man whom Erin immediately recognized walked in front of the fireplace and bowed deeply as though he were in front of a large audience. He nodded to his left, and to

Erin's utter astonishment, she heard the dissonance of a symphony orchestra tuning up! Slowly the tuning sounds of the instruments ceased, the young man raised an invisible baton and gave the downbeat to his unseen musical fellows. The opening measures of orchestral music swept through the shop. Noah left his position as conductor only long enough to play solos on the restored piano in the corner. Erin half expected finely dressed concert-goers to become visible, seated among the plants, whispering and nodding approval. When the music finally stopped, she felt overwhelming admiration and wonder for Noah's musical gifts.

"Erin Grimly, this is Noah Sebastian, my junior partner." Mr. Gather smiled in amusement as Erin walked over to Noah and very shyly handed him his book.

"Does Miss Rob know you can do that?" Erin stammered.

Noah gave a hardy laugh. "So, you are one of Miss Rob's students. I knew I had seen you today. But I've been so many places in the last ten earth hours, I couldn't fit you into the proper scenario. To answer your question, Erin, Miss Rob does not know I can do that." He closed his eyes. Music filled the air. Erin stared in wide-eyed amazement. "Actually, that can be a bit of a problem at times. I just think too hard about a

music score, and all my brain waves spill over into the atmosphere. So far during my lessons with Miss Rob, I've successfully controlled it."

"Do you play Bach two-part inventions?" Erin asked suddenly, her mind travelling back to the barn's mystery music of a few days before.

"Mr. Sebastian," Mr. Gather interrupted, "if you're back in control of your musical brain waves, I could use your magic fingers at my desk."

Noah smiled mischievously at Erin without answering her question and strode to Mr. Gather's beautiful eighteenth-century desk. He began assessing the pile of correspondence stacked there.

"Erin, would you wash the door windows and polish the door frames in the back while I work on the locks?" Mr. Gather asked. "Saturdays are slow, and I need to make a few minor repairs."

Erin went back to the apothecary section to get some wood polish, window cleaner, and a couple of clean rags. Finally, after assembling everything she needed, she walked to the back and started polishing the Family Door's orange exterior.

The furniture polish smelled delightfully of lemons and wax. The job went quickly, and she soon found she had progressed to the mysterious purple door at the end of the row. She decided to tackle the windows before the door frame, and reached high over her head to get at the topmost pane. Parenthesis came over and sat beside her, purring softly. Erin briskly wiped the dirt from the two top panes, turned her rag over and prepared to attack the dirty middle ones. Parenthesis abruptly stopped her contented purr and emitted a low growl.

"Why, Parenthesis! What's the matter? Don't you like the smell of window cleaner?" Erin smiled at the cat's sudden change of mood. She reached down to scratch the feline's ears. Parenthesis hissed and swished her tail angrily back and forth, moving away from Erin's outstretched hand.

"Mr. Gather? Could you come here, please? Something's upsetting the cat."

Mr. Gather called back in a muffled voice from behind the closed Family Door. "One minute, Miss Grimly. This lock is stuck."

Erin turned back to her windows just as something moved behind the glass and made her jump. "Oh, come on, Erin. You're afraid of your own shadow." She rubbed away at the grime, turning her cloth again. Suddenly, she saw an angry face staring back at her from the other side of the door. It pushed closer to the glass, its animal-like expression of torment now face to face with Erin. Parenthesis yowled and spat with rage. Erin yelled, dropped everything, and ran.

6
Tea Break

NOAH CAUGHT HER by her shoulders as she dashed past and swung her around.

"Erin! What's happening?" He looked into her frightened eyes.

Mr. Gather came hurrying to Erin's side. "Miss Grimly, are you all right? What happened?"

"Mr. Gather—a face—I saw a face in the window. And the cat—she—Parenthesis acted all upset. Oh, I'm sorry. It scared me." Erin felt foolish now that the initial shock was over. Mr. Gather looked meaningfully over Erin's head at Noah.

"That's the second time this has happened, Noah. Last week we had a similar occurrence. Our Mrs. C. thought she saw someone looking in from the other side of the purple door." He turned to Erin. "Can you describe the face, child?"

Erin closed her eyes and concentrated. "No, no, I can't. I only saw it for a second. I had the impression it was a boy's face, though. And I do remember dark hair. But the light was dim . . . I can't be sure."

Mr. Gather walked back to the purple door, leaving Noah and Erin standing at his desk, and stared through the windows into the beyond. "Well, he's gone, whoever he is." Quiet hugged the three as they contemplated the possibilities which might lie beyond the door's windowpanes. Mr. Gather's brisk voice broke into their reveries.

"Miss Grimly, how would you like some tea? Clerks have tea breaks, you know."

"Apprentice clerk, you mean, Mr. Gather. Yes, I would like a cup of tea."

"Good. Miss Grimly, I've watched you working, and you fit in at Antiques, Antiquities, Inc. very nicely. Mr. Sebastian travels extensively at present, investigating possible shop acquisitions. I need a reliable young person like you to help me keep things running smoothly."

Erin felt a smile come inside that glowed warm down to her toes.

"Mr. Gather, I want to stay very much."

"Good. Now, let's sit down to tea. Noah," he turned, "would you be so kind as to finish up the doors? I'm sure Miss Grimly has had quite enough surprises for one day."

Noah went to work in the back while Mr. Gather walked to the apothecary's row of bottles, canisters, and powders. He took down a red and gold rectangular tin. With a silver teaspoon he carefully measured four heaping spoons of tea leaves into a handpainted china teapot.

"Miss Grimly, would you bring me the hot water from the fireplace? Here's a potholder. Be careful. The kettle's been on the fire awhile."

A copper kettle hung from a wrought-iron arm which swung over the fire. After studying the apparatus for a moment, Erin discovered a small hooked pole which she used to pull the wrought-iron arm toward her. The kettle was then within easy reach. Erin carried the steaming kettle to the shopkeeper who carefully poured the scalding water over the leaves in the china pot. After letting the tea steep exactly three minutes, he filled three demitasse cups with the piping hot, fragrant brew. Noah joined them, and they sat down in front of the flickering fire.

"For all sustenance we give thanks." Mr. Gather raised his cup heavenward, lowered it to his lips, and sipped slowly. "Ah, there is nothing like a good cup of tea after an afternoon's work. Sugar, Miss Grimly?"

Erin spooned sugar from a silver sugar bowl into her cup. She took a tiny drink of tea. The pleasant spicy flavors of cinnamon, oranges, and sugar combined with the dark flavor of tea leaves to make a rich drink.

"Well, Miss Grimly, before the terms of your employment are finalized, your parents must give their full consent. I assume you are preparing to tell them . . . soon . . .?"

"Yes, sir. I've called a family meeting for tonight."

The afternoon was almost over, and Erin remembered that she hadn't given the expectant mother cat her snack. She walked over to the antique ice box and reached inside for the container of bat brains. A tail and a pair of ears and whiskers were visible, waiting patiently by the fireplace. Erin picked up the snack dish, spooned the bite-size morsels into it, and delivered them to the waiting whiskers. Glancing at the clocks on the east wall, Erin saw it was time for her to leave.

"Mr. Gather," she called, "it's almost five o'clock. I mustn't be late for dinner."

"Have a good evening, Miss Grimly. God go with you." Mr. Gather opened the door for her, setting the bell jangling.

Climbing the fence and the rockpile wall in the waning light was not going to be easy. Erin hesitated at the rusty wire. To her surprise, there was now a small bridge of steps where she usually had to find a toehold. "Mr. Gather, I don't know how you do these little things, but I'm glad you do!" she laughed to herself and hurried over into her own yard, down the slope to her back door.

Back in the antique shop, Mr. Gather added a log to the smoldering fire. Noah checked the day's receipts at Mr. Gather's desk. Only Parenthesis saw the strange face reappear at the window of the purple door and stare evilly into the little shop. But the purple door was locked, and the face had to remain on the other side for now.

7
Of Rings and Guardians

ERIN SAT DOWN to dinner with her mind full of what she wanted to say and how she wanted to say it. The wonderful smell of frying hamburgers wafted from the kitchen. Ordinarily she would have been impatient for the meal to begin. Tonight, however, she felt the need for as much extra thinking time as possible, and even added a silent plea for assistance as her dad prayed.

Richard Grimly sat forward in his chair, took the top off his hamburger and carefully stacked the layers of condiments he usually added. As he reached for the pickles, he spoke to Erin, "And how is Miss Rob these days? Does she still have all those cats?" The question was asked with a certain amount of distaste. Richard Grimly was strictly a dog man.

Erin smiled at her father. "Miss Rob is fine, Dad. And, yes, she still has all those cats."

Her dad's brown eyes met hers and twinkled back.

"What are you working on this week? I saw some Bach in the studio. How are you and J. S. getting along?"

"Okay! I really like those two-part inventions. They're fun to play." Erin reached for the potato chips.

"I understand from your mother that you've called a family meeting for after supper." Her father looked inquiringly in her direction.

Erin felt her stomach do a little flip. "How about sooner, Dad, like during dessert?"

"Sounds good to me. Pass the ketchup, please."

When the hamburgers had been eaten and the dessert served, the Grimly adults were ready to hear from Erin.

"Emily, Erin, I call this family meeting to order," said Mr. Grimly.

Erin took a deep breath. Her parents looked at her expectantly.

"Mom, Dad," Erin announced in her most businesslike voice, "I have the opportunity to work part-time after school at a little antique shop. A Mr. Gather has set up shop in the barn behind the house, and he's offered me a part-time job as a sales clerk. Think of how much quicker I could afford contacts!" Erin stopped and waited for her parents' reactions.

"Mr. Gather? Not Mr. Zacharias Gather?" asked her mother in surprise.

"Well, yes, I think his first name is Zacharias. Why? Do you know him?"

"Erin, your Grandfather De Jong and a Mr. Zacharias Gather were close friends when I was your age. How old is your Mr. Gather? Mine would be at least seventy-five by now."

Erin thought a minute. How old was Mr. Gather? He didn't look as young as Noah, but he certainly didn't look anywhere near his seventies, either. "I guess he must be older than forty but younger than seventy-five."

"Well, then, it couldn't be the same man, but maybe they're related. I don't even remember what business my Mr. Gather was in—he and Dad were often talking about things way over my head when I was around." Mrs. Grimly picked up her coffee cup and sipped from it slowly, looking off into space, her face suddenly somber. "They both belonged to some special group, as I recall, and wore identical rings. I used to trace the pattern of Dad's with my finger when we were in church. I wonder what happened to it? I don't remember it being mentioned at the reading of his will. Does your Mr. Gather wear an unusual ring?

"I don't remember, Mom."

Mrs. Grimly drank from her coffee cup again and sighed. "I miss my dad, that's for sure, which reminds me: I haven't heard from Mother today. She usually calls before Erin's bedtime."

"Erin, your mother and I need to discuss this together before we give you permission to work.

One of us should meet this Mr. Gather and take a look at the shop before anything is definitely decided. I suggest we temporarily adjourn this meeting until after your bath. That will give your mother and me some time to talk." Mr. Grimly smiled in Erin's direction. "Contact lenses are motivating you to join the world of the working sooner than I had expected," he teased.

Erin got up from the table and headed for the kitchen with her plate. She turned as she came to the swinging door and faced her parents. "Mom, Dad, I really want this job. And, you know, it's not just for the money. I can't explain it. There's something about the shop and Mr. Gather that seems to be sort of calling me . . ." Erin stopped talking and went into the kitchen. Her parents looked thoughtfully after her and then at each other.

"Richard, if her Mr. Gather turns out to be anything like my Mr. Gather, 'we are in for quite a ride,' as my father used to say." She looked meaningfully at her husband.

Saturday night was bubble bath night, and Erin always took a book and a cup of cocoa with her in the tub. Tonight she couldn't concentrate on the pages knowing her parents were discussing her future, so she put down her book and sipped the hot chocolate. She was idly wiggling her toes amid the bubble mounds when she saw a thick white tail and two white ears mirrored in the bath water. Looking up, Erin saw Parenthesis lying contentedly on top of the wicker clothes hamper next to the tub.

"You nut!" she whispered. "How did you get in here?" The cat yawned, rolled her now visible body to one side, and shut her eyes.

"Erin, time to get out. Come into the living room when you've brushed your teeth so your father and I can talk to you." Her mother's voice startled her from the hallway outside the bathroom door.

"Okay, Mom. I'll be out in a minute." Erin climbed out of the tub and reached for her towel. "Parenthesis, you're on my towel. Come on, get off! I need it." She pulled the towel, and the cat whirled around, shook her head hard, and began licking her fur back in place.

"Erin, are you talking to yourself?" Her mother's voice came through the closed door.

"No, Mom." She looked frantically around for a place to hide the big white cat. But Parenthesis solved the problem herself. With a yawn and a long stretch, she disappeared.

Erin gave a sigh of relief, put on her pajamas, brushed her teeth, and went to the living room. Her heart was pounding.

Her dad was sitting in his chair, reading the newspaper. Her mother was working on her latest counted cross-stitch project: a beautiful peach-robed angel with wings unfurled, blowing a brass trumpet.

"What did you decide?" Erin asked in a small voice.

"We've decided, Erin, that since I have a class Monday afternoon, your mother should go with you after school to meet Mr. Gather and see this place for herself. If she thinks this antique shop is an appropriate place for you to work, then you may accept the job. Your mother and I both think it would be an excellent opportunity for you to learn a little bit about the business world."

Erin jumped up, hugged her dad, ran and hugged her mom, and spun around several times on her toes. "Oh, thank you! Thank you! Mom, I know you're going to like Mr. Gather. Oh, and Noah might be there. He's Mr. Gather's junior partner—he plays the piano, Dad, and he—" Erin stopped herself mid-sentence. She decided she would let Noah, the shop, and all its oddities

present themselves to her mom. She couldn't begin to explain all that happened there.

Kissing both parents good night, Erin walked cheerfully to her bedroom, closed the door, and turned off the lamp next to her bed. The room was filled with the green glow of the Nightus Lightus plant. As she snuggled down into her pillows and pulled the blankets around her shoulders, she turned on her side and looked out the window into the night. The trees beyond her windowpanes looked foreboding without their leaves.

Windows.

Erin shivered as she recalled the afternoon's unpleasant incident at the purple door. She huddled deeper, clutching her blankets tightly about her, and closed her eyes. The tea had been delicious. She concentrated on this pleasant memory as well as the delightful anticipation of her mother's visit to the shop, and drifted off to sleep.

8
Sunday

ERIN AWOKE THE next morning to the sound of music filling the air. Her father always started Sunday morning off with some kind of church music, be it spirituals, hymns, or classical selections.

She and her parents arrived at the little stone church just as the Sunday school crowd was gathering. Erin slid into the seat next to her friend Connie, who was red-eyed and red-nosed, holding a large box of tissues in her lap.

"Boy, have I got something to tell you," Erin whispered to her sniffing friend. "You won't believe what happened to our clubhouse!" Erin glanced up and saw Mr. Mosley, the Sunday school superintendent, frowning at her. She immediately looked to the front. Finally, as the group disbanded to go to various classrooms for the Bible lesson, Erin had a chance to talk to Connie.

"So, Erin, I'm dying of curiosity. What's going on at the barn?" Connie sniffed and pulled a blue tissue from the box.

"Well, first, how are you feeling? You look terrible."

"Thank you very much," Connie said sarcastically. "Never mind how I feel, girl, tell me about the barn." Connie sneezed and sighed. "I am so sick of blowing my nose," she added under her breath.

"Connie, the barn has been made into an antique shop. A Mr. Gather and a Mr. Sebastian work there. There are all kinds of things for sale there—even plants! You'll have to come see it. I might be working there . . . if my mom approves of it. She's going with me to the shop on Monday." The girls stopped talking again as the Bible lesson started.

After class, Erin followed her parents down the center aisle of the small sanctuary and sat next to her mother at the pew's end. She settled back against the wood, looking around this room she knew so well. She liked the look and feel of the smooth dark wood pews. The orange frosted-glass windowpanes, with their repeating circular pattern, were calming somehow. She glanced at the faces of people passing her pew and tried to see those sitting in the rows in front of her. She wanted to see who was sitting behind her and started to turn her head, but her mother's gentle pressure on her knee stopped that. She decided to study her bulletin instead.

Just as the organ prelude began, Erin's attention was caught by a large straw hat boasting a sweeping feather. She looked to see who was wearing it. It was Mrs. Chloetilde. On more than one occasion Erin and Arnold had spied on the old lady to see if there was any truth to all the rumors about her that were passed down from older to younger siblings through the years. The children had learned several things of interest. For one thing, Mrs. Chloetilde talked to herself . . . and even answered her own questions. Actually, that was how Erin and Arnold had gotten into trouble the last time. Mrs. Chloetilde was having a particularly heated argument with herself when Erin, who was crouching with Arnold below Mrs. Chloetilde's kitchen window, had a sudden fit of giggles. The two children were discovered and their actions reported to their parents. Arnold's punishment was lenient: one night of no TV. Erin's punishment, however, was more severe. She had to apologize to Mrs. Chloetilde, and she was grounded for a week.

Mrs. Chloetilde sat down in a pew several rows in front of the Grimlys, her feather bobbing in the breeze created by the ceiling fans. She was a rather large woman, and Erin was disappointed to discover that her view of the pulpit was now almost completely obscured. Maybe she could see between the shoulders of Mrs. Chloetilde and the gentleman who was sitting beside her. With a start, she recognized Zacharias Gather. Erin turned to tell her mother.

"Mom," she said in a low excited voice.

"Yes, dear?" Mrs. Grimly was reading the announcements and only half minding what Erin was saying.

"Mom, Mr. Gather is sitting with Mrs. Chloetilde."

"That's nice." Her mother continued reading.

"Mom, listen to me." Erin put her hand on her mother's arm, and she stopped reading to look into Erin's eyes.

"Mom, look at the man sitting next to Mrs. Chloetilde and see if he is the same Mr. Gather you knew."

Mrs. Grimly tried to see the man sitting ahead of them. After a few seconds, she shook her head. "Sorry, Erin. I can't see his face. After the service we'll get a good look, okay?"

No, it wasn't okay, but Erin knew it was the best she could hope for. Worship began, and Erin tried to concentrate on the words that were spoken, the prayers that were prayed, and the hymns that were sung, but she couldn't help watching the back of the man sitting with Mrs. Chloetilde.

As soon as the service was over, Erin eagerly looked ahead of her to the pew where Mrs. Chloetilde had been sitting. Mrs. Chloetilde and her companion, surrounded by a crowd of other people, were going out the door in the front of the sanctuary with their backs to Erin and her parents. Erin sighed with disappointment. Her mother gave her a sympathetic look and steered Erin out the back door to shake hands with the pastor.

9
The Meeting

ON MONDAY ERIN'S body was at school but her mind was at Antiques, Antiquities, Inc. All day she kept checking the round large-faced clock in front of Miss Ryan's classroom. The hands crept slowly around the face, almost as if time had somehow slowed down to a crawl. She and Connie walked part of the way home together, and Erin told her more about Antiques, Antiquities, Inc. As they parted company at Erin's house, Connie promised, between nose blows, to try and visit the shop soon.

Erin hurried up her driveway, jumped the steps to the back porch, and let herself into the kitchen. Her mother was just pouring a cup of coffee.

"Hello, sweetie!" Her mother came forward to give Erin a hug. "How was school?"

"Long! Mom, are you going to drink that entire cup of coffee before we go and meet Mr. Gather?"

Mrs. Grimly laughed and said, "Well, I guess not. Come on, let's go." She put a saucer over the steaming mug and reached for her sweater hanging on the back of a kitchen chair.

Erin ran out the back door, down the cement

steps, and up the flat stones leading to the horse apple tree. She waited on the topmost stone for her mother. Mrs. Grimly came quickly after Erin, and the two joined hands and walked to the back fence.

"Look, Mom. Mr. Gather put this little bridge of steps over the fence for me so we don't have to climb." Erin led her mother over the bridge—three steps up and three steps down.

"Now, this next part is really neat. You see, the front door doesn't open unless you finish the verse on the plaque." Erin stopped in front of the white entranceway and looked expectantly at the gold sign.

Questions, questions,
So much to ask.
Look for the answers
To finish the ____.

"Task," said Erin firmly. The door swung open, ringing the bell overhead. Erin walked ahead of her mother and called out, "Mr. Gather?"

For a second, she was afraid no one was there. The clocks ticked on the east wall. The fire in the fireplace snapped and crackled. Just as she turned to see what her mother thought of the shop, a voice called from the book stalls.

"Erin! You're early today. I was just trying to put these volumes in some type of order." Mr.

Gather came across the room toward them, his upper body hidden by the towering stack of books he was carrying. "People who come to book hunt should not have to work so hard at it."

The tower was leaning precariously to one side. Erin hurried forward to grab for the top texts. Reaching up on her tiptoes she caught two of the books as they were falling to the floor. Mr. Gather put the rest on the corner of his desk and turned to Erin and her mother.

"Mr. Gather, I would like you to meet my mother, Mrs. Emily Grimly." She turned to her mother to finish the introduction and was surprised to see tears in her eyes and a look of shocked surprise on her face. "Mom? Mom, are you all right?"

Her mother smiled a little. "Yes, yes, Erin, I'm fine. Mr. Gather?" She walked slowly, questioningly toward him to shake his hand. "Mr. Zacharias Gather? You look enough like the Zacharias Gather that was my father's friend thirty years ago to be his twin! Surely . . ." she stopped.

"And you, Emily De Jong Grimly, have grown into a fine woman with a fine daughter." Mr. Gather spoke the words gently. "Your father was a good friend." The words hung in the air. Erin looked from her mother to Mr. Gather and back again. There seemed to be more passing between them than just words.

"Erin, why don't you show your mother around the shop while I make some tea? Then we can sit down and talk."

Erin led her mother excitedly from one section to another. Her mother listened and smiled mechanically at all Erin said, her gaze frequently travelling back to Mr. Gather who was in the apothecary corner.

"Tea time," called Mr. Gather after a few minutes.

Mrs. Grimly sat down opposite Mr. Gather and accepted a cup of tea from him. After taking a sip, she sat back more comfortably and said, "Mr. Gather, forgive me for being somewhat taken aback, but you look the same to me today as you looked thirty years ago when I used to talk to you in my parents' living room." She continued to look at him in puzzlement.

"I remember those talks well, Emily. You really gave me a mental workout with all your questions."

Erin couldn't stand waiting a moment longer and burst out, "So, Mom, since you already know Mr. Gather, don't you think it's all right for me to work here?" She waited for what she hoped would be a positive reply.

"Erin, I'd like to speak with Mr. Gather privately, if you don't mind. Is there a corner of the shop where you could browse while we talk?"

Mrs. Grimly looked questioningly around the shop until her eyes found the piano in the corner. "Why don't you play the piano while we chat?"

"May I, Mr. Gather?" Erin asked eagerly.

"Certainly, Erin. There are two keys that stick, but enough of them work to make the sound fairly musical. Noah has been restoring it."

Erin left the two adults sitting by the fire and made her way over to the keyboard. The small keys felt strangely rough under her fingers after having spent most of her practicing life on the slick lacquered plastic keys of modern pianos. She decided to skip exercises today and go right to the good stuff. A little Bach in the barn might be fun again, and this time she would know where it was coming from. She started to play the wonderfully intricate measures and was soon lost in the workings of the little piano. She did not hear most of the conversation between Mr. Gather and her mother.

"So, Emily De Jong Grimly, how is your mother? I have not seen the dear woman in a long time."

"She's fine, Mr. Gather. She has adjusted fairly well to being alone since Dad died. She'll be delighted to know I have found you again. You and Dad were so close. You know, the last time I saw you was at Dad's funeral service . . . that was a long time ago . . ."

"At least twenty years, I think," said Mr. Gather softly. "There was such rejoicing in Heaven that day, too. Your father has quite a few friends there."

Mrs. Grimly looked into the fire and was silent. Erin's Bach repertoire had been exhausted, and she had begun playing some hymns.

"Why have you come back, Mr. Gather? Or, better yet, why did you leave so soon after Dad died? Mother would have had a much easier time of it if you had stayed around." She spoke questioningly, almost accusingly.

"The King sent me elsewhere," Mr. Gather said simply.

"And let me guess," laughed Erin's mother suddenly, "the King has commanded that you return." She relaxed in her chair, her hostilities put aside, and mused privately as to what this could mean.

Mrs. Grimly's gaze fell on Mr. Gather's hands. "I see you're still wearing your ring."

Mr. Gather looked surprised. "You remember about the ring?" he asked.

"You and Dad belonged to some special group, as I recall, and everyone in it wore identical rings." Mrs. Grimly searched her memory for further information. "He died before I really grasped what that was all about," she finished, regret in her voice. "Mother was never willing to talk to me about it."

Mr. Gather looked at Mrs. Grimly and studied her face as if he expected to find answers written on the lines of her brow. He got up, stoked the fire with the brass poker and sat back down again.

"Your father was, and I am, a part of a group of individuals called Guardians. Each member of our group has taken a pledge of obedience and service to the King. We serve Him using the gifts and abilities He has given us. The ring we wear is a symbol of that pledge." He stopped and slid the ring on his left ring finger off and handed it to Mrs. Grimly. She held it gently, tracing the sign of infinity and the dove winging its way skyward in the center. How often she had traced that pattern on her father's ring. . . . "Mr. Gather, I don't know what happened to my father's ring."

"Your mother has it. She is keeping it . . . for now." He looked at her with urgency. "I must talk to you about Erin." The piano's soft music filled the shop. Erin was having a wonderful time playing everything she could think of to give her mother and Mr. Gather adequate conversation time.

"Well, I think my husband will certainly agree to her working here once I tell him that I know you. And this shop looks like an intriguing place to work." Mrs. Grimly let her eyes wander around the perimeter.

"Good. But there is something else we must discuss."

"You just pay her whatever you feel is right," said Mrs. Grimly somewhat hurriedly.

"Emily," Mr. Gather said softly. Her eyes met his, and she sighed deeply.

"It's because of Erin that you're here, isn't it?" She looked across the room at her daughter.

"Yes, Emily. Erin has been chosen to take her grandfather's place in the Guardian circle. She has only to accept it, and the place is hers for the time she is here on earth. Her gifts are many, Emily. That is why I am here, to teach her how to use them for the Kingdom."

Erin had finally run out of memorized pieces and had come quietly back into the fireside conversation. She heard only part of Mr. Gather's last sentence.

"Teach me what?" she asked with interest.

"Mr. Gather, why don't you come over for dinner one night this week? I'll invite Mother, and we can continue this discussion then."

"Teach me what?" Erin persisted. "And may I work here, Mom?"

"Yes, as far as I am concerned, you may work here," said Mrs. Grimly. "How does Thursday evening sound, Mr. Gather? My husband has evening classes on the other nights."

"Teach me what?" asked Erin a third time in exasperation.

"Thursday is fine."

"Oh, Mom, can Noah come, too?" Erin suddenly remembered the young musician.

"Yes, certainly. Say around six, Mr. Gather?"

"I will be looking forward to it." He rose as did Mrs. Grimly and the reluctant Erin. "Erin, you decide with your parents what days would be best for you to come. I personally would appreciate Mondays, Wednesdays, and Saturdays, but that is entirely up to them." They walked toward the front door. "Time-wise, 3:30 to 5:00 would be most helpful."

"Actually, those are good days and times for us, too," Mrs. Grimly answered. "What do you think, Erin?"

"Sounds great to me . . . Teach me what?" she asked one last time.

Both adults laughed. Mr. Gather opened the door for them, ringing the overhead bell. Mrs. Grimly turned to Erin and said, "You are in for quite an adventure, I think." She put her arm around Erin's shoulders and hugged her close as they walked toward their own backyard.

"So, Mom, isn't that the neatest place? Every time I'm there I discover something new I didn't see the day before. And I can't believe you know Mr. Gather." Erin stopped suddenly and turned to her mother. "But, Mom, Mr. Gather doesn't look anywhere near seventy-five years old."

"No," chuckled Mrs. Grimly, "no, he doesn't. But then," she said more to herself than to Erin, "*he* wouldn't." She looked off into space over Erin's head. "Come on, girl, let's go in and plan the menu for Thursday night's company. Race ya!"

The two dashed down the hill and pushed, laughing, into the house.

10
The Covenant

THURSDAY AFTERNOON WHEN Erin came home from school, she was met at the door by the wonderful fragrance of beef in wine sauce simmering away in the crockpot. Closing the back door quickly behind her, she walked over to the ceramic pot and was just about to lift the lid when her mother's voice came from the dining room.

"Don't lift the lid, Erin. Too much heat will escape."

"Mom! How did you know I was going to do that?" She left the pot, and pushed open the swinging door into the dining room where she found her mother putting the finishing touches on the table already set for their company. The simple blue stoneware plates and silver flatware gave such a comfortable, homey impression.

"Why don't you get your practicing out of the way and do your homework. I'll need you later for last minute stirring and pouring."

Erin was anxious for the company to come. Her mother and father had been discussing her all week when they thought she was out of earshot. Erin had caught very little of the conversations and only knew her parents were talking seriously about Mr. Gather, her grandfather, and her job at Antiques, Antiquities, Inc.

She finished studying her spelling words for the next day's test just as her mother called her.

"Erin! Your dad is here with Grandma. Why don't you be the greeter. I'm starting the rice. I'll need you in about five minutes."

Erin's grandmother, a medium height, slender woman, came sedately up the sidewalk and carefully managed the three high cement steps up to the front door with Mr. Grimly protectively at her side. "Well, Erin. How's my favorite granddaughter?" She bent forward and gave Erin a hug and a kiss.

"I'm fine, Grandma. I guess Mom has already told you about my job?"

"She certainly has. And I am so pleased to hear Zacharias Gather is your boss. He *is* still coming to dinner tonight, isn't he?"

"Yes, ma'am. He should be here any minute. Mom said Grandpa De Jong and Mr. Gather were good friends when she was my age."

"Oh, my, yes. Zacharias and Jan were quite a pair." She smoothed back her silver hair and pushed up the long sleeves of her blouse. "Where's your mother?" she asked, changing the subject abruptly.

"I'm right here, Mother," came a voice from the kitchen. "I was just *stirring* and *pouring* . . ."

“Uh, I think that’s my cue,” said Erin sheepishly. She got up and walked through the swinging door into the kitchen. Her mother handed her the wooden spoon for stirring the simmering rice.

Just then the front door bell chimed. A moment later, Mr. Gather followed Mr. Grimly into the room.

“Zacharias! Zacharias Gather! It *is* you!” Grandmother De Jong rose with some difficulty from the sofa and came to the center of the room to meet her old friend.

“Emmie! How wonderful to see you again!” He gave her a warm hug and a kiss. “Let me look at you . . . still wearing those stylish tweeds, I see.” The two stepped apart to get a better look at one another.

Before anything more could be said, Erin came into the room. “Hi, Mr. Gather! Where is Noah?” She looked around hopefully.

“Noah is at the shop. We had another little incident this afternoon . . .”

“The purple door? Did you see that face again?” Erin asked in a low voice.

“Yes. Noah and I both thought it best to leave someone ‘on guard,’ as it were, until this purple door mystery is resolved.”

Mrs. Grimly came through the swinging door carrying the steaming beef mixture in a bowl. “Dinner, everyone! Oh, Erin, I forgot the butter. Would you get it, please?"

When Erin came back through the swinging door she was startled to hear her grandmother use Mr. Gather's very words when she had first met him at Antiques, Antiquities, Inc.

"So, Zacharias, you are still 'a keeper of things old, older, and oldest?'"

"Oh, yes. You will have to come to the shop. I know Erin would love showing you around." Mr. Gather winked at Erin. After the blessing was said, the parade of food began.

"Are you an independent dealer, Mr. Gather?" Erin's dad asked as he reached for the rice.

"No, actually, I have always worked under the auspices of the King." Mr. Gather looked not at Mr. Grimly, but at Mrs. De Jong.

"Oh. The king of England?"

"No, the King of the Universe."

Mr. Grimly stopped mid-chew.

"So, Emmie. Tell me what you have been up to since I saw you last."

Mrs. De Jong looked at Erin and smiled. "I have been heavily involved with my family, Zacharias. I have had the joy of watching my daughter's daughter grow into quite a young lady." She paused and concentrated on her plate for a moment. "And you, Zacharias? What have

you been up to? Where have you been?" She said it in a tone bordering on accusation.

Mr. Gather broke a roll and buttered it. "The Guardians have been busy, Emmie," he said softly. "The enemy is advancing at a far greater rate of speed in this century than in any other in recent history. I have been . . . working . . ."

The room was strangely silent. Erin looked from one face to another, trying to find a clue to the meaning of all she was hearing, and some of what was being left unsaid. Her mother looked puzzled, serious. Her grandmother looked angry. Mr. Gather seemed to radiate a hard resolve, and her father was listening with the same intensity she had seen during concerts he especially enjoyed or sermons he found particularly thought-provoking.

"Yes, well, I'm glad you have come back into our lives, Mr. Gather," said Mrs. Grimly with something of a forced smile.

"I, too," said Mrs. De Jong with sudden conviction, "because it can mean only one thing." She threw a piercing gaze all around the table, as if to draw a conclusion from them on what she had just said.

"What's that, Mother?" Mr. Grimly looked questioningly at the older woman.

"That this family is once again being called to join the battle!"

Erin didn't know what to think. This was not the way she had envisioned dinner with Mr. Gather. She had expected some interesting discussion, but this conversation certainly left her in the dark.

"Are we ready for dessert?" Mrs. Grimly asked.

"It's pistachio cake, and it's good. I already had a little piece," Erin confessed. The adults around the table laughed and the mounting tension seemed to dissolve. Erin helped her mother clear the table of the dinner dishes while Mr. Grimly brought out the cake, coffee cups, and forks.

"Mother, all this talk of Guardians has reminded me of something. What ever happened to that ring of Dad's? The one with the infinity sign and the dove in the middle?"

"I have it," her mother answered shortly.

"Oh, good. I was afraid it had been lost."

Mrs. De Jong put down her fork and sighed. She tugged on a silver chain around her neck until it swung free of her clothing. The ring was suspended from it. She removed it from the chain, and set it reverently next to her plate. Erin lost all interest in dessert.

"Why don't we go into the living room and finish our coffee there? Richard, perhaps a little music . . .?" Mrs. Grimly left the question unfinished and looked at him confidently.

"Grandma, may I see Grandpa's ring?" Erin sat next to her grandmother on the sofa and snuggled up to her. Wordlessly, her grandmother handed her the silver chain and ring.

"What is a Guardian, exactly?" Erin asked. The silence that met her question had an almost tangible quality. She looked to her grandmother and then to Mr. Gather. So did her parents.

Mr. Gather put down his coffee cup and cleared his throat. "A Guardian is an individual who promises to love and serve the King with all his heart, mind, and soul; and to love his neighbor as himself."

Erin looked thoughtfully at the adults around her. "The King is Jesus, right?" she asked the question softly.

"Yes," said Mr. Gather.

"Well, then, wouldn't that description fit everyone sitting here?" she asked.

"Yes and no," said Mr. Gather, stroking his chin. "I think I can safely say everyone in this room acknowledges Jesus as King and God's Son," he gazed at the other adults seated around him. Then he looked back at Erin. "But the commitment to Kingdom service is different for each one of us. A Guardian's commitment is to 'front-line' service, as it were. A Guardian hears the King's call and leads others to action." He stopped and let the words sink in. "A Guardian is often a protector—as I protect the Doors. I also teach—in that way I am a protector of truth. Your grandfather was a doctor, a Guardian of health and wholeness."

"And you are here tonight to tell us who has been called next to wear the Guardian ring and join the circle of the Guardians?" Grandmother De Jong looked squarely at Mr. Gather.

"Yes, I am."

In the silence that followed, Erin looked from one face to another, trying to get some hint of understanding from the people around her. All she could feel was the sense of seriousness of it all. Looking finally at Mr. Gather, she found he was looking directly at her.

"Erin Elizabeth Grimly, in the name of the King, I ask you to join us in the circle of Guardians." He spoke the words in measured tones, each phrase weighted to the comma.

Erin was incredulous. "Me? You want me to be one of these Guardian people? You've got to be kidding!" She looked down at the ring in the palm of her hand. It glimmered in the lamp light. She was surprised when her grandmother put her hand over Erin's and pulled it into her lap.

"Erin," she said, "your grandfather was very much like you. He loved people, music, his work.

But most of all he was a Kingdom seeker, as you are now. He wore the ring of Guardian with the conviction that Kingdom work was the best work to be doing. I think you would be a wonderful Guardian."

"I'm just a kid! There's nothing special about me!" Erin turned sober eyes on Mr. Gather. "I'm not brave enough to do this. You know I'm afraid of shadows," she said, remembering the face behind the purple door.

"Being afraid is no reason for refusing a guardianship, Erin. But it is not something to be accepted lightly, either. Suppose we leave it like this: you take some time to talk to your mom, dad, and grandmother; pray about this, come talk to me if you like, but you must make your decision by Monday."

"That's only four days!"

"I know, but the King is giving you more time than He gave some fishermen who worked for him . . ."

Erin was excited, scared, and confused all at the same time. She looked at the ring again.

"Okay, I'll come and tell you Monday what I have decided, Mr. Gather." She thought for a moment. "Mr. Gather, what would my Guardianship be? Would I be a doctor like my grandfather?" She didn't like the sight of blood, and screaming babies got on her nerves.

"Your Guardianship will become apparent as you grow in fellowship with the King. He has not told me what you will become."

Erin slipped the ring on her finger. It was much too large, and she spun it around and around. "I'll tell you Monday, Mr. Gather." Then she added more to herself than to the group around her, "Wait till Connie hears about this!"

11
A Joyful Event

ERIN ROSE FROM the couch, gave the ring back to her grandmother, and said good night to everyone.

"Come get me when you've brushed your teeth, and I'll tuck you in," said Mrs. De Jong.

Erin walked to her room, closed the door and fell across her bed. A white tail was resting on her pajama-pillow. Undoubtedly, Parenthesis had come for a visit.

Her eyelids growing heavier by the minute, Erin got into her green-striped flannel pajamas and snuggly warm bathrobe, brushed her teeth, and then went to get her grandmother. Peeking through the door into the living room, she hoped to hear more about this Guardian business. Her mother saw her and spoke.

"Good night, honey. Sleep tight."

"I'll see you Saturday, Erin." Mr. Gather said.

Grandma De Jong got up, came through the door, and stood next to sleepy-eyed Erin. The two of them walked arm in arm to Erin's bedroom only to find Parenthesis completely materialized but fast asleep on Erin's down comforter.

"That's Mr. Gather's cat, Grandma." Erin climbed under the covers, stretching her toes down toward the ice cold foot of the bed. She lay back on her two pillows, sinking into the delicious softness.

Her grandmother sat down on the edge of the bed, smiling at her granddaughter. When Grandma De Jong smiled, her whole face filled up with the light of it.

"Grandma, I want to know more about Guardians, and the ring and —"

"Whoa, hold on. I think you've heard enough serious talk for one day. Saturday, I'm sure our Mr. Gather will tell you more. Good night, honey. Sweet dreams."

The Nightus Lightus plant glowed in the darkness. Soon Erin drifted off to sleep, with Parenthesis stretched on the comforter at the foot of the bed.

Erin was dreaming about music and parades when she woke with a start and sat up in bed. Squinting hard to see the numerals of her clock radio, she saw it was only 2:00 A.M. Just then she felt a push against her legs. Looking down, she saw Parenthesis lying on her side, with a tiny, newborn kitten searching for his first meal.

"Oh, no! She's having kittens in my bed!" Erin carefully slid over the side of the bed and thought for a moment about what she should do. She hurried toward the kitchen phone. *Phone!* Erin thought frantically. *I've never even seen a phone in Mr. Gather's shop. Should I wake up Mom and Dad? No,* she said to herself, *I'll just go and get Mr. Gather myself.* Erin hastily put on a coat over her night clothes. Shoes in hand, she moved quietly to unlock the kitchen door and stepped outside.

Everything seemed different in the moonlight. Somehow even the distance through the backyard seemed farther. Erin was so excited and in such a rush that the shadows and pockets of darkness frightened her only a little. She stopped short at the rockpile. "What am I doing?" she said aloud. "It's two in the morning. Mr. Gather won't be at the shop at this hour." She felt panic rise within her, and the shadows loomed larger and more suggestive. Erin ran to the shop's front door. "Emergency—open, please. Erin Grimly here." The door swung open. Much to Erin's relief, Mr. Gather had been dozing in his big chair in front of the fire, a book in his lap, and he sat up with a start when the overhead bell rang.

"Mr. Gather, Mr. Gather," Erin gasped, "Parenthesis is having kittens!"

"Child, child, calm yourself. She is an experienced mother . . . What time is it?" He sat up in his chair and looked at the clocks on the east wall.

"But Mr. Gather, you don't understand. She's having them . . . in my bed . . . right now!" puffed Erin.

"Oh, my. We'd better get there right away."

Erin soon found herself walking through her own bedroom door with Mr. Gather behind her. They had no time even to catch their breath before the room was filled with the sound of a French horn fanfare.

"Did you hear that? I heard trumpets!" Erin looked quite startled.

"No, no, my dear Erin. Those sounded like French horns to me."

Erin looked at Parenthesis again. "Two of them! I see two. Look." Sure enough, there were now two sleek black kittens snuggling against their mother's fur.

Suddenly, the royal fanfare sounded again, and beside Parenthesis lay not one, not two, but three solid black shapes of hungry fur.

Mrs. Grimly walked into Erin's bedroom looking quite disturbed just as the horns sounded the fourth time. Her eyes searched the room from ceiling to floor, but of course nothing was there.

"Erin! Mr. Gather! What in the world . . . ? Did you hear French horns?"

"Mom," Erin broke in quickly. "Parenthesis is having kittens in my bed, and Mr. Gather has come to get them."

A possible source of all the noise suddenly came to Mrs. Grimly. "I know who's making all that noise—Arnold Lorenzo! He's always up to something. That boy—blowing his horn at this hour. I'm calling his mother first thing in the morning."

Mr. Gather and Erin looked away from each other so they wouldn't laugh. After twenty minutes had passed with no additional arrivals, Mr. Gather said, "Well, Erin, it looks as though there won't be any further additions to the family tonight. Mrs. Grimly, would you be so kind as to make a loan of your laundry basket and Erin's comforter so I can get my new family home?"

"Oh, certainly, I'll get the basket for you." Erin was stroking Parenthesis gently when a

new sound filled the room—the very unmelodious noise of an off-key foghorn.

"Mr. Gather, that wasn't a very musical announcement."

"How curious!" was all Mr. Gather said.

"One, two, three, four . . . five! But Mr. Gather, look. This latest one is greyish, and he's so little compared to the others." She bent down for a closer look.

At that moment, Mrs. Grimly re-entered with the wicker basket in one hand and a small saucer of milk in the other.

Parenthesis carefully disconnected herself from the five hungry mouths, strolled over to the milk, and lapped it hungrily.

Mr. Gather gently gathered up the comforter, kittens and all, and placed it in the wicker basket.

"Mrs. Grimly, thank you so much for your kindness. I'm sorry your sleep was interrupted. Erin, I'll look forward to seeing you Saturday afternoon. Good night." He picked up the basket slowly so as not to jostle the occupants. Erin followed him into the hallway and showed him out the back door, holding the screen door open for him.

Mrs. Grimly came up behind Erin, putting her arms around her in a hug. "How about some sleep, night owl? You have school in the morning, you know. And Erin," she said more determinedly, "I'm definitely going to call Arnold's mother in the morning. Practicing at this hour —the nerve of that boy!"

Erin grinned and choked down the laughter she felt tickling its way out of her throat. Here her mother was, standing right in the middle of some kind of supernatural event, and she thought it was Arnold.

They said good night a second time and Erin got into bed. Closing her eyes, she felt a glow of happiness: kittens, and five, too! Too tired to think of another thing, she sank into a deep sleep.

12
Intruder

ALL DAY FRIDAY, Erin kept thinking about Guardians, the new kittens, and the choice she had to make. Several times during the day she had the opportunity to talk to Connie about the events of the night before, but something held her back. Erin walked home alone since Connie's big brother had basketball practice, and Connie had to wait for him. Practicing Bach two-part inventions only made her feel more muddled than ever today, so she went upstairs and started reading a mystery to get her mind focused on other things for a little while.

Her mother came to tell her that supper was ready only to find Erin sound asleep in her chair. Erin woke up Saturday morning—astonished to find herself in bed and in a new day.

Early Saturday afternoon, Erin walked to her piano lesson. She was disappointed when Miss Rob greeted her alone on the front steps. What was Noah up to? At 3:28, she headed up the hill to Antiques, Antiquities, Inc. The front door was tightly closed, and she read the poem on the rectangular plaque expectantly.

To grow, to learn, or just to be,
The challenge today is
Enough for _____.

"Me," said Erin firmly. The door opened. Taking a deep breath, she walked in. "Mr. Gather? Hello, I'm here." Erin called.

"Erin! Hello! I'm dusting books—be with you in a minute. Take a look at the kittens. They're in that big box by the fireplace. They've outgrown your mom's laundry basket already."

"Kittens? Did I hear someone mention kittens?" A voice came from the back of the shop between the Doors and the bookshelves. Distracted, Erin turned to see a pair of brown leather shoes coming down out of the ceiling followed by trousered legs slowly descending an invisible spiral staircase. It was Noah.

"Hi, Erin! How are those piano fingers?" Noah looked teasingly in her direction.

"Noah," Erin gasped. "Where did you come from?" She still shocked easily over the seemingly impossible happenings that occurred at Antiques, Antiquities, Inc. on a regular basis. "I missed seeing you at Miss Rob's."

"I was upstairs, resting—I only just arrived from Ceylon. Here, I brought you something." Noah pulled a flat, medium sized box out of the air and handed it to Erin. She opened it eagerly. Resting in the tissue paper was what looked like a long piece of cloth.

"What is it, Noah?"

“It’s called a sari. The women of Ceylon wear it like you wear a dress. The only unfortunate thing about this present is that it doesn’t come with directions. I really don’t know how they take one piece of material and wrap it around themselves so that it stays on all day.” Noah turned to his partner, “I’d like to discuss some possible acquisitions with you. I saw the most interesting . . .” The two men moved toward Mr. Gather’s desk and continued talking together.

Erin settled on the Persian rug to peek at the kittens. She was amazed to see how much they had grown in just forty-eight hours.

The peace of the shop was suddenly broken by the sound of shattering glass and the security alarm.

“Quick, Noah! Get Erin out!”

Noah steered Erin out the front door. Then he rushed in again. The alarm stopped blaring a moment later, but neither Mr. Gather nor Noah came out to get Erin for some time. Finally, Mr. Gather stepped outside.

“What happened?” Erin asked.

“It looks like someone or something tried to break into the shop through the purple door,” Mr. Gather said.

They walked back inside the shop to the doors, where Noah was busily boarding up the broken pane with a rectangular piece of plywood.

"Better check the lock, too," said Mr. Gather after he helped Noah install the glass. The job completed, they stood back.

All at once, Noah yelled, "There! Did you see it? Look! A face!"

Erin saw for a second time the face on the other side of the purple door. It was an angry face glaring out at them from a deep grey background. The face came closer to the glass, and Erin could make out uncombed black curly hair framing a pale visage. Clenched fists rose out of the darkness and looked as though they were going to smash yet another glass pane. But then the being and his fists moved farther and farther away from the windowpanes, until finally there was no sign of him at all.

"His door must have rotated past our entrance," said Mr. Gather. "Well, I must say this is quite unusual. Noah, are you getting anything?" Mr. Gather looked questioningly at the younger man.

Noah looked into the dark nothingness beyond the wood frame door. "I hear very sad music, Mr. G., a sadness from the depths of that creature's very soul. He is troubled and wants to escape." Noah's eyes closed, and his slender fingers reached out to a glass pane as if to draw knowledge from it. Very softly at first, and then building to a dramatic crescendo, a melancholy sonata spilled into the room. The sadness of it swept over Erin.

"That is his song," said Noah after the music ceased. "He feels that way very often . . . And he is only a boy-child."

Erin didn't speak. Somewhere deep inside her own soul, she had heard some bars of that music, felt a small measure of that sadness. It was the music heard when one lost something or someone very precious. She sighed deeply, wishing she could have reached through to the clenched hands now gone on the other side of the door.

13
Two Headaches

MONDAY AFTERNOON FINALLY came. Erin arrived at the shop after school, somewhat breathless from rushing and from the knowledge that she was about to commit to an adventure that could take her almost anywhere. Today a verse was waiting for her:

Make a joyful noise
unto the Lord
All ye ______.

Finishing the verse with "lands," she was grateful her third-grade Sunday school teacher had helped them all memorize Psalm 100.

Mr. Gather was sitting by the fire, reading from a small leather-bound volume.

"Good afternoon, Erin." He looked at her with serious expectancy.

"Good afternoon, Mr. Gather." She had so much to say she didn't know quite how to begin.

Mr. Gather motioned wordlessly to the chair next to his.

"Mr. Gather, I've thought it over very carefully, talked to my parents, and prayed about the Guardianship. I've decided to accept it."

With the words barely out of her mouth, Erin was startled by the sound of rushing wind and looked up to see a dove flutter beside her, holding a rolled piece of parchment in its beak. The dove dropped it in Erin's lap and flew into Mr. Gather's outstretched hands where it nestled comfortably. Erin unrolled the scroll with trembling fingers and read aloud:

On this day of January,
The High Council has noted in the King's Book
The acceptance of the sacred trust of Guardian
Passed from Guardian Jan De Jong, M.D.,
To Erin Elizabeth Grimly, a child of the covenant.

Erin looked in amazement at Mr. Gather. He walked to the front door and opened it, tossing the dove gently into the air, shielding his eyes as he watched it wing its way homeward. After a moment he rejoined Erin by the warm fire. He sat watching her thoughtfully, his head tilted slightly to one side and resting against the palm of his hand. Erin became a bit uncomfortable, wondering exactly what he was thinking. She had expected something more upon her acceptance of the Guardianship—*like a French horn fanfare?*

"I am glad, Erin, very glad," he said finally, then got up and stirred the fire. "We will start your education at once. There is much to learn, and even though your age is in our favor, we must not waste time."

"Mr. Gather, when does a Guardian get the ring? I certainly can't wear my grandfather's. It's way too big for me."

"The ring . . . yes . . . ." He sat back down in his chair. "Guardians are coordinated or directed, so to speak, by a group of elected officials called the High Council. The Council decides when the ring of the Guardians should be awarded once a Guardianship has been accepted."

"Oh," said Erin with some disappointment. "You mean I have to wait?" She hadn't counted on that. "There's no chance I could get it today?"

Mr. Gather laughed. "No, I don't think you will be getting it today, little one. However, the High Council will not dangle it out of your reach for long. They are simply waiting to see if you have really committed to this endeavor with your whole heart. Once they are sure of that, you will find the ring on your finger. Now, why don't we get some shop work done."

Erin took one last look at the document in front of her, rolled it up again, and slid it behind her on the chair. She got up and one of the four black kittens leaped out to frighten her, then scampered away. The kittens were growing at an amazing rate, developing at a speed well out of the earthly range of zoological parameters. Erin watched now as they pounced on each other, twisting and rolling head over paws, chasing tails, and running to Mother when their games got too rough. Erin noticed with concern that the little grey kitten seemed slower than the black ones.

"Mr. Gather, explain the kittens to me."

"This is only the second litter of kittens Parenthesis has had since her arrival from behind the purple door; therefore my knowledge is rather limited. The four black kittens already are displaying extraordinary abilities. In just a few weeks, they'll have mastered the use of their power of invisibility, their power to grow greater or smaller with the twitch of a whisker, and they will be able to travel interdimensionally."

"But won't the grey one be able to do those things?" Erin gave Harold, the omnivorous conifer, a mist bath while she spoke.

"No, Erin," Mr. Gather said thoughtfully. "I'm afraid not. Of course, Foggie may be able to do some of these things in varying degrees, but he isn't like the others. He was born last, the runt of the litter, and weak, I'm afraid. He'll be quite earthbound compared to his brothers and sisters."

Erin felt sorry for the kitten whom she had named Foghorn in remembrance of his unusual birth announcement. She looked around to find him. The front bell jangled, diverting her attention, and she turned to see someone standing in the door, wrapped from head to toe in

Make a joyful noise
unto the Lord
All ye lands

a heavy patchwork quilt. Black patent leather shoes poked out from the bottom edge. A large hat with a sweeping red feather perched on top. The hat Erin immediately recognized. This had to be Mrs. Chloetilde.

"Zacharias, I have a splitting headache. Do you have anything for it? Some tea, perhaps? Oh, my aching head." A moan came from the upper folds of the blanket.

The quilt moved in awkward jerks and twists to Noah's chair by the fireplace. The shoes propped themselves up on the fireplace fender. It was hard to believe there was a body under all that wrapping.

Mr. Gather hurried forward, a look of concern on his face. "Erin, get the jasmine tea tin. You'll find it behind our regular brand." He sat down next to the elongated bundle of fabric.

"Maude, dear, tell me what happened."

Mrs. Chloetilde sniffed loudly, and Mr. Gather extended his handkerchief. In just a few minutes the jasmine tea's sweet aroma filled the room, and Erin carefully brought the tray of chinaware to Mr. Gather.

"Maudie, please, now here's some tea. Tell us what's wrong," Mr. Gather coaxed gently.

"Oh, Zacharias, it's my son, Maurice, Jr. He, he, he . . . oohhhhhh." The quilt was quivering, and both black shoes kept getting less and less visible as it slid over them. "Maurice, Jr., wants to put me in a retirement home. He says I'm not safe alone." Here Mrs. Chloetilde really started sobbing.

"Maude, I know Maurice. He'd never say a thing like that, unless of course, oh Maudie, you didn't . . ." Mr. Gather gave the quilt a meaningful stare.

"Zacharias, it was an accident. I promise, on my honor, it was an accident. I was fine tuning my satellite dish yesterday, and all I could get was static on my TV screen. Last week I'm sure I got Mars, you know . . . Then that little snoop Arnold Lorenzo looked in my front window and scared me so badly that my fingers pushed four or five buttons at once. That blew my color TV set to smithereens!"

"And then?" said Mr. Gather.

"And then this big clap of thunder crashed outside, and lightning flashed in Arnold's face, and he ran away, screaming something about witchcraft, of all things!"

In her mind's eye, Erin could see Arnold running down the street, the victim of a sudden thunderstorm. The thought of it was too much for her, and she tried without much success to stifle her laughter.

"Now, now, Maudie. Don't worry. This was obviously an accident."

"Oh, Mrs. Chloetilde," chortled Erin. "I wish I'd been there to see that! Uh, I mean . . ." She stopped short as the quilt swung around to afford its wearer a better view of Erin.

"Maude, this is Erin Grimly. She works for me now. Erin, Mrs. Maude Chloetilde. She has been a shop patron for a number of years, and she is a good friend besides."

Erin held her breath. This could be unpleasant if Mrs. Chloetilde chose to bear Erin a grudge after their last encounter.

"We've met . . . briefly." Erin was relieved to detect no hostility in the words, though she still couldn't see Mrs. Chloetilde's face hidden behind the quilt.

Very slowly, Mrs. Chloetilde let the quilt slide down and with one hand hugged it close around her shoulders. Mrs. Chloetilde's eyes were red from crying, and her nose was scarlet from blowing. She poured herself another cup of tea, settled back, sighing deeply. "But Maurice, Jr., is right," she said softly. "I'm not safe. Who knows what might happen next?" A tear slid down her cheek.

"Maude, I'll talk to Maurice. I have an idea. One of Parenthesis' kittens isn't going to be as powerful as his siblings. Maybe if he were around to watch out for you, Maurice would change his mind."

Mrs. Chloetilde put down the cup she was holding, and a smile spread across her face. "Really? Oh, Zacharias! A kitten. I've been without a pet for ages," she continued wistfully, looking directly at Erin for the first time.

"Erin, find Foghorn and let Mrs. C. look at him."

Erin started her hunt for the little grey feline. Foghorn came sauntering around the row of potted plants, and then pounced on an invisible nothing. Erin scooped him up and held him close to her face, getting tickled by his ever-active whiskers and prickly pink tongue. She walked to Mrs. Chloetilde's side and carefully handed her the kitten.

"Ohhh, Zacharias! He's precious. What beautiful green eyes! But, Zacharias, a cat can't take care of my mistakes."

Foghorn sank his claws into the quilt and climbed up to the woman's shoulder. He sat there squinting his eyes and smiling.

"Maudie, Foghorn can't undo your mistakes, but he can come over and get Noah or me, or even Maurice, Jr., if you'll show him where we all live."

Big tears began to roll down Mrs. Chloetilde's cheeks again, but this time she was smiling. "Well," she sniffed, "that certainly makes me feel better, Zacharias."

Suddenly, Mrs. Chloetilde leaped up. "Oh, no! I left dinner in the oven! My baked potatoes will be burnt to a crisp!" She loosened Foghorn from her shoulder, gave him a kiss on the nose, and set him down. "I'll be back, sweetie!" She ran out the door, leaving the quilt in a heap in the chair. Mrs. Chloetilde turned and yelled over her shoulder, "It was nice to meet you again, Erin."

Erin walked over to Mr. Gather, put her arms up around his neck as high as she could reach, tugged his head down a little, and kissed him on the cheek. Mr. Gather smiled in mild surprise.

"What was that for?" he asked teasingly.

"You know what it was for, Mr. Gather. You care so much about people. You listen, and then you think of a plan to help. I want to be like that."

Erin turned and gathered up the cups and china pot, and walked to the apothecary sink to rinse them out. She filled the basin with soapy water and plunged in with both hands. When the bell jangled as the front door opened, Mr. Gather went to welcome their latest customer.

The noise of the steady stream of rinse water drowned out the sound of voices, and when Erin finally turned the faucet off, she found she was listening in on the middle of an argument.

"I told you, Miranda Banushta, no one uses the purple door until I, as Guardian of the Doors, have explored it completely."

"Guardian! Ha! *You*, old man, are nothing but a washed-up janitor! I want the door now. Do you hear me, Gather?" Miranda's voice rose in a screeching crescendo.

"There's power behind that door, Gather. Power different from anything I've ever experienced. I want to know more about it. Now! Do you hear me?"

Erin came out from behind the shelves just in time to see Miranda pull her rectangular panel from her pocket and press one of the buttons.

Thunder rolled, lightning flashed, a mighty wind ripped through the shop sending glassware smashing to the floor, books whizzing helter-skelter against the walls, and plants bending almost to snapping against the force of it. Erin had never seen anything so terrifying in all her life.

Mr. Gather walked slowly toward Miranda, his eyes flashing in anger. He held up his ring hand, palm turned in, the ring glowing brighter and brighter. Parenthesis stood near Erin, back arched in anger, with a hiss and a howl coming from deep in her throat.

"I am Guardian of the Way," Mr. Gather repeated slowly. The ring seemed to come alive with a brilliance all its own. Miranda covered her eyes, but Mr. Gather didn't even blink. Light flashed and flickered as reflections bounced off the shards of broken glass scattered over the shop floor.

From behind her hands, Miranda spoke menacingly, "I eventually get what I want, Gather. Nothing can stand in my way." She began fading quickly and then was gone.

Erin came from the apothecary section trembling, tears brimming in her eyes. She ran to Mr. Gather, who knelt down next to her and silently gave her his handkerchief.

"It's all right, Erin."

"But she was so angry," choked Erin. "And she is so powerful—oh, Mr. Gather, please don't fight with her again. She could hurt you or even, or even—" Erin couldn't finish the sentence.

He put his hands on her shoulders and looked gently into her eyes. "Today you've learned two, really three, very important axioms in the teachings of the King. First, you must stand absolute on the facts and duties you know to be the Way, to be right as God tells us. Second, you must always do the very best you are able for your neighbor, as we did for Maude. And third, the power of a mortal like Miranda is nothing in comparison to the power given Guardians by the King. Miranda is the one who should be afraid, not you!"

Erin still felt very frightened and angry.

"Why didn't you just zap her one then?" she asked in tearful vehemence.

"That would have been a waste of one of God's gifts to me. I was safe enough." The calm voice gave Erin a sense of reassurance.

"How does she know anything about what's behind the purple door?" Erin asked.

"I'm not sure. It would not surprise me at all, however, if Dr. Banushta has researched far beyond her scientific texts this time."

Erin turned and looked at the wrecked shop. What a mess. Glass was all over the floor, and dirt was strewn everywhere from overturned planters. Harold was one of the few things unscathed by Miranda's wrath. He had his branches hugged to himself like a closed umbrella.

The kittens! Where were they? Erin frantically looked around. "Foghorn? Here, kitty, kitty. Come, puss, puss."

Being quite concerned himself, Mr. Gather began searching in the corners, by the woodpile, and under the chairs by the fireside, picking his way carefully through the broken glass, when he looked up and started laughing. "Erin, I think we can stop the search. Look at Harold!"

Harold's branches were slowly unfolding, and down his trunk came five kittens, acting as though nothing had happened. Parenthesis sat down in the midst of them and began carefully licking her nearest offspring.

"Feel better now?" Mr. Gather smiled down at Erin.

"Yes," Erin managed a wan smile.

"Why don't you take Wednesday off? Today was a bit much."

"What? And miss a day of my Guardian lessons or not see the kittens? No, sir. I'll be here Wednesday at 3:30," she smiled. "Precisely 3:30."

14
The Planned and the Unplanned

TIME SEEMED TO have wings during the winter months. Noah was at the shop often, constantly filling the air with melodious strains of piano concertos and an occasional rock tune, which he claimed was to wake up Harold. But Erin quickly learned Noah's little tricks and saw that he was being a tease. Mr. Gather preferred classical music and would start dusting Noah off with his feather duster every time Noah sounded contemporary pieces. "Just have to be sure none of your channels have gotten dusty," Mr. Gather would say.

School days slid by uneventfully. Erin and Connie continued to enjoy each other's company, but both girls sensed growing animosity from Arnold. He seemed angry much of the time and could level a classmate with one of his well-aimed verbal assaults.

After a particularly busy afternoon, Mr. Gather sat down wearily at his desk and flipped open his desk calendar.

"April already? I feel I have known you at least one hundred earth years, Erin, yet it's been only a few months."

Clocks ticking, Parenthesis purring, fire crackling, smells of tea and old things tickling her nose had all become so important to Erin. She was now a part of two worlds, belonging to one, and a frequent visitor to another. But she felt connected to both, a sense of "being in tune," as Noah would say.

The room suddenly filled with music, and Erin turned her gaze expectantly upward to find the source. Noah was just coming down the spiral staircase from the second floor, both of which were still invisible to Erin. If there was a second floor, Erin certainly couldn't figure out where it was.

"Noah, Erin, I have a rather unusual announcement to make." Mr. Gather sounded pleased with himself. "Friday and Saturday Maude and I are going to go door-hopping! She has talked me into a cruise on the Victoria III, and I'm looking forward to the diversion."

"Oh, Mr. Gather! You'll love it!" said Erin.

"Does that mean Erin and I will be in charge?" Noah grinned conspiratorially in Erin's direction.

"No. That is the rest of my announcement. I'm giving you both the time off. We've all been working very hard of late, and as senior partner, I declare a holiday!"

Thursday night, Erin was unable to fall asleep, so she sat up in bed and mentally went through the shop's inventory, hoping to lull herself to sleep. Parenthesis lay in a white heap on the side of her pillow, purring. Erin reached out a hand to stroke the long, silky fur.

No shop work Saturday, she thought sleepily. Her mind slipped slowly into complete quietness. But calm did not follow her into sleep. Her night was filled with dreams of breaking glass, opened doors, clanging alarms, and a feeling of danger. The next morning she awoke feeling tired, and grouched her way through most of the day.

After school, Connie caught up with her. "Are we still sleeping over at Anne's tonight, grumpy?" she asked teasingly.

"Yup. I'm taking a nap first, though. I'm tired."

"Okay, kid. I'll meet you by the antique place—that way we can walk together to Anne's house. Bye, there's my brother." Connie ran ahead to catch up with her big brother who paid her two dollars a week to carry his books as well as her own, all the way home.

"What time?" Erin yelled after her.

"Seven. I have to wash dishes tonight," Connie yelled back.

"See you later then!"

Erin walked the rest of the way home alone. Once inside, she ate five Fig Newtons and drank a glass of milk, practiced piano thirty minutes, and then fell asleep on her bed. Her mother woke her up for dinner, and Erin felt in considerably better humor.

"Erin, don't forget to pack your toothbrush. And please remember to tell Anne's mother 'thank you' for having you girls over."

Erin checked to be sure she had everything. "Bye, Mom."

"Bye. See you in the morning." Mrs. Grimly held open the door for Erin and watched her daughter walk up the hill of their backyard.

Erin had already crossed the steps over the rockpile fence when she heard Parenthesis howl from somewhere close by. Looking around, she spotted the cat pacing the shingles of the antique shop's roof.

What is she doing up there? wondered Erin. "Here, kitty, kitty."

Upon hearing Erin's call, the cat scampered to the low overhang and leaped to the ground. She ran to Erin, meowing continuously. Erin rested her suitcase and sleeping bag against the side of the shop and reached to pet the cat who scurried past her outstretched hand.

"What's the matter?" Erin called after the cat. Parenthesis scampered in the direction of the shop's front door, growling and hissing.

Erin was surprised to see the front door part way open, and the shop's interior dark, except for the dim glow of embers in the fireplace. A sweeping light beam in the back of the shop illuminated the doors.

"Noah? Noah, are you here?" Erin called in a shaky voice. She stepped into the dark room.

No one answered, and the beam of light was extinguished. Then Erin heard a low moan that sent a chill up her spine. "Lights, please!" she

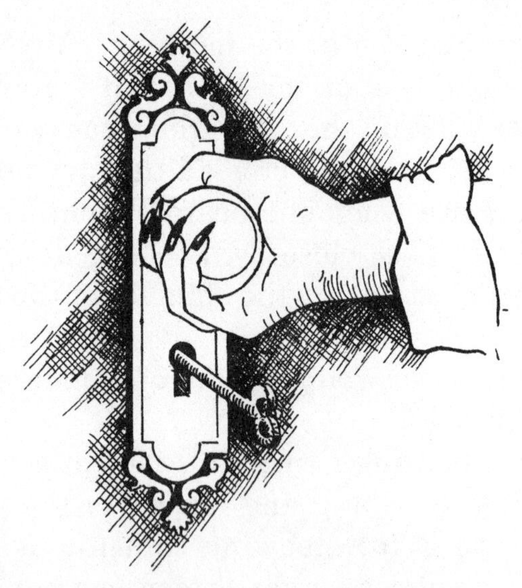

spoke commandingly into the darkness.

The lights blazed, and for a second Erin couldn't see. As her eyes adjusted to the bright lighting, she saw Noah lying face down on the floor by the piano, and Miranda Banushta impatiently twisting the knob of the purple door. Miranda had somehow managed to find a key that fit the lock, and its long stem stuck out of the keyhole.

"Noah? Madam Banushta, what have you done to Noah?" Erin's rage at the thought of her friend being hurt proved stronger than her fear of Miranda's power, at least for the moment. She ran toward the woman, not sure what to do next.

Foghorn shot out from behind Harold, causing Erin to trip, slip, and slide right into Miranda, whose body was already pressing hard against the purple door. The sudden force of the two bodies crashing together was just enough to jar the stubborn frame, swing the door open, and send Miranda and Erin tumbling into the black emptiness beyond.

15
Nightmare

ERIN FELT HERSELF falling through layers of cool, moist air currents. Wind whistled past, brushing her cheeks with long fingers of breeze. She was alone, falling through what she hoped was the atmosphere of a friendly place. At first, she felt high enough to reach out and touch the stars; now, only a few seconds later, she could make out vague copper-colored continental formations below. The ground was coming up to meet her faster and faster. The breezes turned into roaring winds. Fear crept up from her stomach and burst out in a scream.

"Help! Help! Somebody help!"

Erin squeezed her eyelids shut. She knew in just a matter of seconds her body would blend into the strange, brown landscape below her.

But Erin's entrance to this new world hadn't gone unobserved. Protaimeus, one of the area's guardian angels, had been alerted to her plight and came quickly to her aid. He intercepted Erin in mid-air, and the two landed unceremoniously on a sandy hillside.

The hill was crowned with a row of slender, weedy bushes. A hot, dry wind kept their branches in continual motion. Erin felt stray wisps of her ponytail lift as the wind whispered past her.

"Oh, thank you so much! I really thought I'd had it," said Erin breathlessly. She sat up rather uncomfortably on the coarse sand. Looking around, she saw sand in all directions, seemingly an endless beach with no ocean shoreline.

Protaimeus smiled laughingly back at her. "You have forgotten your wings, little bird," he teased. He took a breath and folded his robed arms across his chest. "I was only doing my job. I am one of the guardians of this place." He bowed solemnly, revealing elegant alabaster wings folded gracefully behind him.

"You're a Guardian? Then you must know Mr. Gather. He is a Guardian without wings, though, Mr. . . ."

"Protaimeus. Just call me Protaimeus."

"Protaimeus, you don't have a ring." Erin felt a wave of distrust and confusion pass through her. Granted, Protaimeus had just saved her life, but what could she really be sure of in this new place? Whom could she trust?

"Gather?. . . Ring?. . . I'm afraid you are not talking about things of which I am knowledgeable. But perhaps if you tell me more, I will gain understanding." Protaimeus looked quite patient and sympathetic. His seeming ignorance brought tears to Erin's eyes. She began to realize how serious her predicament was. Mr. Gather had no idea she had fallen through the purple door, nor did Noah. She didn't even know where she really was. And what had happened to Miranda?

"Come," said the angel encouragingly. "Let's walk, and you talk."

They rose and walked along a narrow path among the long-limbed shrubs at the top of the hill. Their footsteps were soft whispers in the sand. "My name is Erin. I am from Zacharias Gather's antique shop, and I'm here by mistake. You see, I tripped over a kitten and accidentally fell through the purple door, and well, here I am." She stopped, feeling her explanation was inadequate and confusing. "Where am I?"

"That is a bit difficult to explain. So, you came through a door. I have heard of the existence of such entrances, but you are the first visitor I've met."

"You know about the door? Oh, good! You can help me get back then." Erin felt much better until she noticed her companion's silence.

"Erin, I don't know the way to send you back, but I shall keep my eyes and ears open." Then Protaimeus seemed to tense slightly. He looked over Erin's head, off into the distance. "In the meantime, you need only to call me if you have need of anything." Protaimeus rose gracefully into the air and hovered over her momentarily.

"Protaimeus, don't leave me, please! I don't know what to do." Tears spilled over onto Erin's cheeks.

"Erin, I am guardian angel to one called Demont. He is one of the broken ones, and I dare not leave him to his own devices for too long. I must go. But do not fear this place. Even the dunes will move for you here if you have faith enough. If you have need of anything," he repeated, "call me . . . call me . . ." The words echoed in the wind, and he was gone.

Erin wiped her tear-stained cheeks with her sleeve and started walking slowly along the narrowing path when she thought she heard voices. Walking faster, she left the pathway and turned in the direction of the sounds. Getting closer, she distinctly heard two voices. One she recognized—Miranda!

"You listen here, boy," Miranda snapped savagely. "You know all about this place, including the way out, and I want to know everything, now!" Erin could see her beyond a dune, but the other speaker was hidden from her view.

"You can't do anything unless I help you," said a whining voice. "And I won't help you unless you help me!" Defiance rang out loud and clear.

"You do as I ask, you little nothing, or I'll use you in one of my experiments in inter-dimensional space travel. You'll never see your family or friends again!" Miranda stepped menacingly forward.

But the other stood his ground. "I don't have a family, and I don't have friends. And besides, wonder-woman," the voice was brimming with sarcasm, "in this desolate hole, your experiments will probably only work in little spurts—if they work at all," he added triumphantly.

"You bratty kid, I landed, didn't I?" She reached into her pocket and yanked out the panel of buttons. She extended it toward the boy and pressed two buttons. Nothing happened. Furious, she pushed several combinations of buttons. Still nothing happened.

Until this time, Erin had not been at the right vantage point to see Miranda's companion. But now the other voice laughed harshly, and the being moved into Erin's view. It was the pale face she had seen through the purple door windowpane!

"Now do you understand? Or does the wonder-woman still want to throw her empty threats at her only chance for education and escape?" The thin lips formed an evil grin, and Erin wished she were light-years away from this place.

"Wonder-woman, there was someone else who came through that door with you. Don't deny it—she stands a few feet behind us. Come forth, girl-sneak! Let me see you at last without a glass between us!"

The astonished Erin stepped forward nervously. "H . . h . . hello," she hiccuped.

"Hmpph. You're plain enough. But two of you—two of you will fit into my plans very nicely. That is, of course, if the girl-sneak wants to go home and is willing to pay the price. Are you?" He leered at Erin, who, by now, was feeling indignation entwined with her fear.

"My name is Erin, not girl-sneak, and yes, I want to go home, but I don't understand about the price. I don't have any money, if that's what you're after." She spoke boldly, stepping toward the boy.

"Stop! Don't come near me! Your earthliness would pollute my genius with a mere touch of your fingers, Erin-sneak."

"All right, I won't touch you, but stop calling me 'sneak.'"

"But you are a sneak. You've been talking to that pest Protaimeus, haven't you? Well? Answer me!" he roared. "I saw you sitting with him."

"So what?" asked Erin, growing more defiant by the minute.

The curly-headed youth came toward her and then stopped. "Protaimeus thinks he can tell me, Demont the Foremost, what to do, where to go. Well, we shall see, we shall see. I have a plan," he stopped himself and turned back to Erin. "But you never answered my first question, Erin-sneak. Are you willing to do a little task for me? I, in turn, will tell you how to get home." Demont smiled winningly at Erin.

Miranda strolled over, looking slyly at Demont.

"She isn't even an adult, so what could she possibly do to—"

"Shut up!"

Miranda backed up two or three paces, snapped her mouth shut, and looked as mad as ever.

Erin spoke. "What would I have to do?" she asked curiously.

Demont looked around and bent forward as if he meant to share a great secret with her. By accident, Erin's hand brushed his pale white one, and he drew back screaming as if in pain.

"I told you, don't touch me! Don't touch me! Are you so empty-headed that you can't follow simple directions?" He stopped short, his face contorted in terror. "Oh, they'll hear me! They'll hear me!" His voice changed from one of rage to one of panic. "I've got to hide. Run! Run!"

He dashed across the sand, leaving Erin and Miranda alone in the small clearing.

"Come on, Grimly-thing. He knows where the exit is. He told me that in three days of this planet's time, the exit won't be usable again for at least four years!

"This is your doing, Grimly-thing," Miranda continued as they shuffled clumsily through the sand. "You pushed me through that door, so now you are going to get me out." Miranda shaded her eyes with both hands. "Drat this bright light. I can't stand it." She was already out of breath. "If you stand in my way, I'll have no choice but to dispose of you . . . permanently!"

Erin's legs had new motivation to catch up with Demont.

"It's no use, we've lost him." Miranda turned on her, eyes flashing. Suddenly a voice whispered, "Here, wonder-woman, I'm here."

Erin and Miranda turned and saw a hand beckoning from behind a large outcropping of boulders. "Bring Erin-sneak. This way. Hurry."

Walking cautiously around a grey rock, they found themselves at the entrance to a dark, uninviting cave. Dim light glowed from within.

"Come in before they see you."

They had to duck to enter the cave's chamber.

"This is my best hiding place. Even Protaimeus hasn't been here."

A fire in the center flickered, throwing long black shadows on the rough cavern walls. Erin could just make out a cot on the far side of the fire with books and loose papers strewn near it.

"Sit down, but don't touch me!" Demont sat uneasily on the cot, glancing nervously at the cave entrance as if he expected an army to march through at any second.

"Demont, we want to go home. Tell us your plan so we can get on with this." Miranda impatiently jerked off her left shoe and poured a stream of sand onto the cave floor.

"Ah, yes . . . the plan . . . the plan . . . my plan." Demont stepped into the light of the fire, grinning evilly. "I could have led them out of this desolate place. I know a way out . . . a way to another world where we could rule and not be ruled . . . where there is no sand, and miles of green, growing, life-giving things; but no, . . . they refused me, Demont the Foremost, and now they watch me all the time. The big watcher is Protaimeus."

Erin broke in, "Demont, Protaimeus called you 'one of the broken ones.' What does that mean? And who exactly is the 'they' you keep talking about?"

"I'm not one of the broken ones! I'm not! I'm not!" Demont screamed wildly. "He lies about me like that all the time." He was suddenly calm again. "He lies, they lie; he watches, they watch. So, I, Demont the Foremost, am going to punish them all for lying and watching." He circled around the little crackling fire and stopped in front of Erin and Miranda Banushta. "There is only one place of green, growing things; only one place of life in this disgusting sandy pit, and I plan to burn it! And you, wonder-woman, and you, Erin-sneak, are going to help me."

He began laughing and laughing until he cried. He hugged himself tightly, staring into the ever-flickering fire. "That will teach them to say no to me . . . they will pay for this," he muttered again and again. "Oh, yes, . . . they will pay."

16
Revenge

AS DAY FADED into evening, Demont easily managed to gain Miranda's cooperation for his plan. Erin, however, was a different story. Her inner conflict was great. Yes, she did want to go home, but getting there by cooperating with Demont in his plan of revenge was not right, and she knew it.

Darkness crept into the cave and was only chased away in snaps and crackles by the little fire. Outside, the stars shone so brightly that Erin could see the sand dunes and a line of distant steep, craggy cliffs. *This place is beautiful at night,* Erin thought to herself.

"Well, Grimly-thing, are you going along with Monty's little plan, or are you staying in this dreadful place for the rest of your life?" Miranda hissed out the words from farther inside the cave.

"It's wrong to help him, Miranda."

"And what gives you the right to be judge and jury? How do you know helping him would be wrong? Maybe he *is* the unappreciated genius he claims to be. I can certainly identify with that. You, on the other hand, are only a child . . . and not a very bright one." Miranda haughtily turned her back on Erin.

Erin felt tired and confused. What did she know to be right? What did she know to be true? She started to cry, wishing her mother would wake her up and tell her she was having a bad dream. Oh, she wanted to go home.

Demont came to the cave's entrance and jerked her roughly back inside. "Watch her," he commanded Miranda. "The girl-sneak knows Protaimeus. She could ruin everything. Protaimeus must not learn of this plan. Not this one!"

Erin wiped her eyes on the sleeve of her shirt. "You've had other plans?" she asked, sniffing.

"Oh, yes, but I don't want to talk about them," he said quickly. "Let's talk about this one." He took a smoking taper from the fire and pointed it at Miranda. "Tell me again what you will do tomorrow."

Miranda smiled conceitedly. Erin felt like throwing up. "On your signal, I am to orchestrate the diversion: a rip-roaring sandstorm of hurricane proportions. My panel has just enough punch to pull that off."

"And you, Erin-sneak, what will you do?"

Erin spoke in a hoarse whisper, "I told you, Demont, I won't help you."

"What?" Demont stood up angrily, the taper held in his hand like a sword.

"I said, I won't help you!" Erin spoke loudly this time, eyeing Demont in a mixture of fear and defiance.

"You'll never get to the exit then. Never! I'll never show you. And Banushta, I'll show you only after your work is done."

"What? After it's done? Forget it! You show me before, Demont, *before.* I don't trust you, you little worm. I'll see it before the caper, or no help will come from me."

"How do I know wonder-woman can give me a storm?" Demont asked suddenly. "Have you lied? Can you really do as you say?" He advanced toward her, the smoking taper in his hand flaming suddenly. "I haven't a chance of setting the fire if you can't make it storm."

In answer to his question, Miranda took the little flat panel in her hand and pressed two, then three buttons. A breeze blew, became a gale, sending papers and bits of the fire swirling into the recesses of the cavern. Thunder crashed outside. Sand whirled in tiny tornadoes on the cave floor.

"Enough! Enough! Protaimeus will come. Stop." Demont began to panic at Miranda's display of power.

Miranda pushed another button, and the wind quieted. She smirked at Demont, then gave Erin a nasty look. "The combination code is different here, but the effect is the same." She put the panel back into her pocket. "Demont, I want to know more about this place. Does it have a name? Who else lives here?" Erin heard an edge of excitement in Miranda's voice.

Demont slumped down by the fire. He sat with his knees pulled close to his chest. "This is the desert, the pit of sand, the abomination of desolation. It has no name with capital letters, if that is what you mean." His subdued tones awoke in Erin new pity for him.

"And the others who live here? What are they like?" Miranda came around the fire to sit nearer the boy.

"They are all idiots!" said Demont with sudden fervor. He jumped up and ran to the cave entrance.

"Come, wonder-woman. I'll show you the exit place. Erin-sneak, you will come along, but not all the way."

The evening air wrapped around them like a warm blanket. As they walked, Erin tried to pay close attention to her surroundings. She soon realized that Demont had out-thought her and was taking them on such a confusing route that as soon as she thought she'd found a boulder or sand dune to remember, she saw another exactly like it.

Miranda came up beside Demont and continued speaking on her earlier topic.

"Demont, I read about a place like this—a desert—that hosted an incredible healing force, a power of immense proportions. Is there such a force here?" Dr. Banushta stopped to rest a minute. She watched Demont expectantly.

"Oh, yes," he said with growing sarcasm, "oh, yes, there is such power here. The Almighty is the holder of it. He wastes it on the others." Demont spat out the words with contempt. He squatted down and balanced carefully, hugging himself.

"Wastes it?" asked Dr. Banushta in feigned innocence.

Demont leaped up and angrily flung a handful of sand at Miranda's feet.

"Yes! Yes! Yes!" he yelled. "He heals those stupid broken ones. He gives sight to the blind. The lame walk. Stop asking questions! You are here to help me!"

Demont turned and sprinted up the path. Erin and Miranda chased after him.

They'd been running for a long time when Demont finally stopped, and the two followers caught up with him. He pushed Erin down so she was sitting on the sand Indian-style.

"Don't you dare follow us, Erin-sneak. We'll be back in a few minutes. And here," he whispered in her ear, shoving something small and cold in her hands. "Hold this." Erin's hand gripped something cold and hard. It felt like a key.

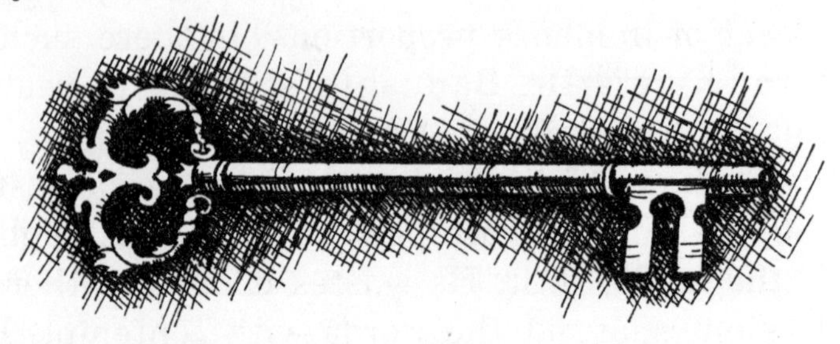

She didn't like being left alone. She started to get up when she heard them already returning. They were arguing.

"Do you think me stupid? Did you really think that I'd show you the whole way out before you helped me? I'm no fool!"

"Demont, you are despicable!" From the way Miranda spat out the words, Erin could tell she was furious. "You'll get your stupid sandstorm. Stop worrying about it. How am I supposed to get that door open?"

Demont only laughed. "When the sun comes up again, and you've begun the storm, I'll tell you how . . . but not until then."

Demont led them back to the cave. He didn't take back the object he'd given Erin. She looked at it quickly. Her guess had been right. It was a key. But why hadn't he taken it back? She slipped it into the elastic band of her kneesock while pretending to scratch her ankle.

They returned in the same crazy way they'd come, zigging and zagging, twisting and turning, leaving one path and finding another—or were they all the same?

"Grimly-thing, do you have any idea what a gold mine we've stumbled into here?" Dr. Banushta's voice was shrill with excitement. "What I could do with power like that on earth! The possibilities are endless!" She was momentarily speechless with exhilaration. Then she spoke softly to herself. "I need time to think. After tomorrow's little mission, I'll return to earth and regroup. Next time I come, I will meet this 'Almighty' and take the power from Him!"

When they reached the cave again, Erin was only too glad to rest her back against the rough rock wall. She thought she'd just fallen asleep when Miranda was shaking her awake again.

"Get up, Grimly-thing! It's time."

"I won't help you destroy anything." Erin's voice was tired but resolute.

Demont pushed Erin toward the cave's entrance. "You have to come along. We can't have you staying behind and warning that pest Protaimeus about what we're up to, now can we?"

None of the landscape seemed familiar to Erin at first, and then it all seemed the same. A sparkling twinkle of azure blue suddenly blazed in Erin's line of vision for a millisecond and then was gone. Was it a mirage? No, wait, there was a blink of green . . . and blue again. They were nearing the oasis, Demont's destination.

A change came over Demont. It was as though a cloud were passing over him, shadowing his features, turning them more pale and evil than ever. He began muttering to himself, wringing his hands nervously. His mouth moved, and Erin heard the words "they," "lies," "revenge" repeated over and over.

"Come on! Let's be done with this! I have things to do elsewhere!" announced Miranda excitedly.

Erin knew there was no hope of turning back now. They followed the path downhill, and around the next bend they were greeted with a full view of the sweeping reaches of the oasis. Palm trees swayed in a gentle breeze, fields of crops reached heavenward. Tents were pitched on the far side of an invitingly cool lake. Sheep, goats, and three camels were penned near the tents. All was serene in the early morning quiet.

"I'll start the storm down there and when it's really brewing, I want that information, Monty, do you understand? I can always stop, you know." Panel in hand, Miranda walked away from Erin and Demont.

The sun was suddenly darkened by clouds

which appeared from nowhere. A rising wind churned the morning air. The plants in the field swayed and bent. Sand blew everywhere. Erin felt its sting on her cheeks, arms, and legs, and quickly shielded her eyes with her hands. Demont reached into his knapsack and came up with three pairs of goggles. He threw a pair over to Miranda and another pair to Erin. Erin got the goggles on just in time to see one of the distant tents collapse and portions of it tumble away. She was afraid for whomever might have been inside.

"Stop! Stop! You'll kill someone!" Erin screamed into the wind. "Protaimeus! Protaimeus!"

"Shut up, girl-sneak, or I'll—"

"Monty," Miranda yelled from a nearby dune, "tell me how to open that door now or all my storming stops."

"All right. You just need the key. The girl-sneak has it."

"The key, Grimly-thing! The key! Give it to me!"

"No! No, I won't! You're horrible, Miranda Banushta, and I won't give you the key—ever!" Erin felt momentarily revitalized. She started running back up the trail, but the wind caught her and slammed her against the side of the cliff. She fell to her knees, the breath knocked out of her.

"Oh, blast! Well, it doesn't matter! I'll just break the glass and reach the knob from the other side." Miranda pushed several panel buttons and disappeared from view.

Demont started screaming, "Stop! You haven't done it all yet. Stop!" Then he turned in the direction of the oasis, and a horrible smile spread over his face. He reached into the knapsack again and pulled out a large glass container filled with clear liquid. He quickly pulled some rags out of his pockets and doused them liberally with the fluid. Running to the outer edge of the oasis, he poured the remaining liquid on several fence posts.

"Protaimeus! Protaimeus!" Erin screamed. She got a mouthful of sand as Miranda's wind roared on. In horror she watched Demont reach into his pocket and take out a book of matches. But when the matchhead scraped across the matchbook cover, there was a soundless explosion, and Demont was gone.

17
Coda

ERIN BOWED HER head, crying. In anger and frustration, she pulled off the goggles and tossed them aside. She was sobbing so hard that she didn't notice the storm abating or the approach of Protaimeus. His feet touched ground beside her. His arms reached out and gently raised her stooped shoulders.

"Erin, Erin. Do not cry." He spoke kindly, reassuringly.

"Oh, Protaimeus. Where have you been? Did you see the storm? And Demont, Demont! I think he's been blown up. He must be dead." She started crying again.

"Erin, look up," Protaimeus commanded. "What do you see?"

Erin raised her tear-streaked face. She looked around in surprise and astonishment. The fields stood unscathed, tents squat and sturdy in the now gentle breeze.

Erin laughed in surprise through her tears. "And the people—are they safe?"

"Quite safe."

"Oh, but what about Demont. There was an explosion. He was going to burn the oasis . . . he's so mixed up, Protaimeus."

"There is so much to clarify for you, Erin." Protaimeus laughed a deep, warm laugh. It reminded Erin of Noah's music. "Demont is safe. The Almighty cares for all His children, especially the broken ones. You show such compassion for one who has mistreated you. That is a sign of greatness in my circle." He paused. "Do not worry about Demont. The Almighty cares deeply for him and seeks daily to bring Demont back into the fold." They sat down under a tall palm tree at the oasis's edge. Protaimeus reached into the deep folds of his robe and brought out a book.

Erin studied its leather cover. It was worn at the top and bottom corners, and the cloth page markers were quite frayed. It looked a lot like one of Mr. Gather's favorites. Protaimeus took the volume lovingly in his hands and turned to a well-worn page. He read slowly, the words sweeping over Erin like a warm wave:

Do not call to mind the former things,
Or ponder things of the past.
Behold, I will do something new,
I will even make a roadway in the wilderness,
Rivers in the desert.

"Those words, Protaimeus, I know them! I heard them last Sunday in church. They are from the book of Isaiah, I think."

"We grow closer and closer every moment," said Protaimeus warmly. "Oh, but I almost forgot my news! The Almighty told me of a door back to your place of origin. But we must hurry a little, for it cannot be used except at certain moments."

Then Erin remembered the key. She pulled it from her sock, showing it to the angel. It gleamed golden in the sunlight.

"You don't need the key," said Protaimeus. "The Almighty will open the door for you."

Erin suddenly remembered Miranda. "Protaimeus, another person from earth is here, too. Demont showed her the door, and she was going to break the glass to get the door open so she could get back to earth. She is going to steal the Almighty's power!"

To Erin's surprise, Protaimeus threw back his head and laughed. "I am not sure what will be done with her, Erin, but one cannot steal the Almighty's power. One cannot pass through that door without the Almighty's blessing, even if one breaks the glass."

"Demont broke the glass once," Erin said half to herself.

"Yes, I was close by. He was not harmed, but he was not allowed to leave. Erin, we must be going. Come. Let me carry you. It's a bit of a walk, and time is short."

The angel picked Erin up. The rhythmic

bend and sway of the angel's wings were like a lullaby to the exceedingly tired Erin. She felt herself falling asleep.

"Erin," a faraway voice spoke. "Wake up! We're here."

Erin stretched sleepily and rubbed her eyes. An outcropping of limestone cliffs rose out of the sand in front of her. She was surprised to see a narrow door set in one of the cliff walls.

After handing the key to Protaimeus, she reached for the knob and found that it turned quite easily. The heavy door swung open slowly as she pulled. Erin took a deep breath and stepped through to the purple beyond. In a matter of seconds, she was stepping into the antique shop, as though her journey had only taken her down a familiar hallway to another room. Noah was sitting in a chair with an ice pack on his head, and Mr. Gather was pacing the floor by the fireplace.

"Mr. Gather! Noah, I'm back! Noah, I'm so glad to see you with your eyes open!"

The two men turned to her, relief flooding their faces. "Erin! Oh, Erin! We didn't know what to think! Foghorn came to get me, and I found Noah unconscious when I arrived, and the purple door open. . . ."

"What day is it?" Erin interrupted in alarm. Her mother and father would be out of their

APOTHECARY
please
ask for
assistance

minds with worry. She had been gone for two days!

"It's Friday evening, Erin," Mr. Gather looked at her, mystified.

"What time?"

"Almost seven," he answered.

Erin walked to the fireplace chairs and sank with great relief into the cushions. She reached out to pet Parenthesis.

"Mr. G., you won't believe what's behind the purple door. It's a land of desert and oasis, and a guardian angel named Protaimeus lives there. Oh, and the face we've been seeing belongs to a boy named Demont—"

The clocks chimed the hour, interrupting Erin's stream of speech.

"Erin! Where are you, kid? Erin! Come on! We'll be late for the party!" Connie was calling her from outside by the rockpile.

"Go now, little one. Tomorrow you can tell us more about what lies behind the purple door. You can even help me write the description for the door now that you've been there!"

"Yes, sir!" she smiled. "Tomorrow, at 3:30, precisely."

Epilogue

Golden light danced and glimmered on the surface of the highly polished Council table. The beings assembled around it ceased their private conversations and turned to hear the words of the gentleman speaking excitedly to the other Guardians around him.

"She stood up to him," he said with glad conviction. "She stood up to that Dr. Banushta, too. Certainly that shows she's got what it takes to be a Guardian." He looked expectantly from face to angelic face.

The angel to his left laughed indulgently. "Yes," he said, "she certainly shows great promise. But the Council's careful consideration and testing is not over yet. We need more evidence of her commitment and growth in Kingdom matters."

The silver-haired man smiled ruefully and sat down. Looking at his ring finger, he said softly to himself, "There's more to come, Erin. Watch and pray, so you will be ready when the next testing comes."